MANHUNT

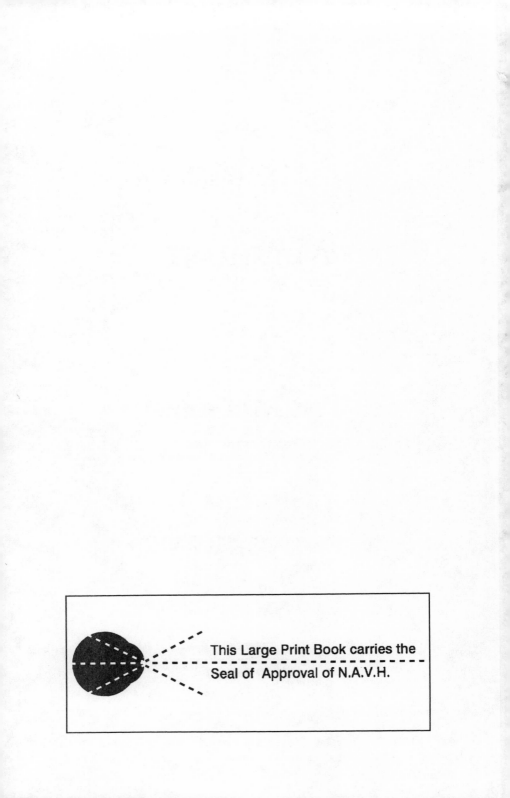

This Large Print Book carries the
Seal of Approval of N.A.V.H.

MANHUNT

TIM MCGUIRE

WHEELER PUBLISHING
An imprint of Thomson Gale, a part of The Thomson Corporation

THOMSON
━━━━✸━━━━ ™
GALE

Detroit • New York • San Francisco • New Haven, Conn. • Waterville, Maine • London

THOMSON

GALE ™

LIBRARY OF CONGRESS CATALOGING-IN-PUBLICATION DATA

McGuire, Tim.
    Manhunt / by Tim McGuire.
        p. cm. — (Wheeler Publishing large print western)
    ISBN-13: 978-1-59722-450-5 (softcover : alk. paper)
    ISBN-10: 1-59722-450-2 (softcover : alk. paper) 1. Large type books. I.
Title.
    PS3563.C36836M36 2007
    813'.6—dc22   2006035182

Published in 2007 by arrangement with Leisure Books, a division of Dorchester Publishing Co., Inc.

Printed in the United States of America on permanent paper
10 9 8 7 6 5 4 3 2 1

To the Readers of the Rainmaker:
The multitudes that have contacted me
and those I have yet to meet, who won't
let this character ride off into the
sunset.

ACKNOWLEDGMENTS

Thanks to the Travel Montana Tourism Organization for the geography. And as always, the camaraderie of the DFW Writer's Workshop, without which this writer would be alone with his lonesome tales.

Atop the wooded rise, he took a deep breath and let it go, all the while staring at the shack below. Smoke billowed from the stove stack, carried to the east by the soft morning breeze. Two unsaddled ponies nibbled at spring grass in a corral of gnarled tree trunks. With no barn or other shelter in sight, there wasn't any cover for a shooter to hide. Thick white clouds made for a checkered sky of sunlight. More clouds on the way meant less shadows to be cast before open windows. Rain was coming too, but not until nightfall. There wasn't much time. The bounty hunter who had tracked him across the country for over six years was inside the shack. There was a promise to keep.

He steered the palomino down the short, sheer slope to avoid the front and approach from the west. Once on level ground, he slowed the horse to a walk. No need to startle the ponies or those inside. At the edge of the shack, he quietly slid from the saddle and, before he took a step, considered why he had come to Montana.

If he didn't rid himself of the bounty hunters, they would continue to dog him every place he went for the rest of his life.

Memories as a Kansas farm boy, war drummer, cavalry soldier, trail scout, and finally guide in for the army expeditions into the northern nations were bittersweet. The few good ones were mostly forgotten since the day Custer charged down that valley to the Greasy Grass. After that, white folks knew him only by his ma's favorite moniker, the Rainmaker. This is why he traveled to Montana. To put an end to it.

A groan came through the wall. Someone was directly on the other side. He gradually drew the Army Colt .45. Cautious steps put him to the side of the shack. More groans came faster. The sound of a woman in pain. He'd been bit before by barging into the business of others, but he couldn't ignore the deep cries.

He leapt to the raised porch. Just poking his head in the doorway could get it shot off. He pulled the latch and kicked it open. Reflex had him point and cock the Colt at the first thing moving. The black man in the bed threw up his hands.

CHAPTER ONE

"Don't shoot! Cole? That you?"

Cole eased the hammer to rest. Taking in air, he sized up what he'd done. In the bed was the man he'd come to see, lying atop some squaw years shy of the same age. The fear in her face appeared directed at the pistol pointed at her and not at the naked man under the same sheets. He exhaled, figuring he had been bit again.

"My mistake," Cole said, quickly drooping the revolver to his side. Feeling a need for a sack to put over his head, he mumbled his embarrassment. "I guess you all know each other. I'll wait outside. Don't mind me. I'll be fine. Take your time."

He closed the door, shook his head, tucked the Colt into the hip holster, and stepped off the raised porch. The edge he'd rode for so long had cut into his judgment once again. A smirk creased his face when he thought about what he disturbed, then he heard the creak of the door behind.

"Howdy, Choate," he said as he turned to meet the man.

The half-breed came out wearing only pants held up by suspenders over brawny shoulders. "You knock?"

Cole nodded. "Yup, I know. I feel a fool for not."

"Should." Choate came off the porch and stood head to toe, the same as Cole. A moment passed before both broke their firm faces with laughter.

"Ain't nothing to stop a man in the middle like a gun aimed at him," said Cole. "Feeling poorly about it. From what I heard, she was in an awful way. Had I known you took in a squaw, I might have figured what was happening in there before I busted in. Must be true what's said about you people." Choate slowed his laugh enough for Cole to see the matter was more personal than first thought. "She your woman?"

Both men looked back at the shack. "Is now. She's Crow. Lost her brother near a year ago. Killed in a tribal skirmish. Never belonged to a man. I took her." He faced Cole. "Didn't see you first with whiskers." Cole rubbed the beard grown by two months in the saddle. "Then I saw the hide leggings," Choate continued. "Then the black shirt. Like it's your skin. I never seen you out of it."

"It's green. Just looks black." Cole noticed a slight change in the wind and the aroma of food. "Could use a meal, if you got any food to spare."

Choate nodded. "Come inside. She cooks good, too."

They went to the house, Cole keeping a step behind even when entering. The woman now stood in a corner, having wrapped herself in a dress of skinned hides. Her black hair lay in tangles that hid most of her face. Although she wasn't white, he removed his hat in respect for a woman's home. She peeked into his eyes, constantly dipping hers away as if not wanting to stare.

Choate gestured to her and pointed to Cole. "She is Silent Owl. Deaf. Tribal elders told she was sick when young. Nearly dead, but when she woke, she not hear their words."

Cole nodded to her and gestured his understanding to Choate. It was easy to know why her tribe abandoned her. A woman who couldn't work as well as others and needed extra care was no prize to keep.

When he closed the door, he saw the table hidden behind it. Choate invited him to sit. Both men settled on the raw wooden chairs

14

as Silent Owl took two roasted birds from the small hearth spit.

Cole looked to the half-Crow, half-colored man who had hunted him from Kansas to Idaho. The features were the same as his father's. Cole dipped his eyes away. Each appeared ill at ease to speak first, but the bond between them rivaled that of cousins.

"You are good for coming here."

Cole shrugged as Silent Owl brought the food to the table. "It was you that trusted me." He twisted a bird leg free, as did Choate. "Seemed only right for me to return the favor. Besides, you are the only one I can count on not to shoot me in the back."

"Did you find the people for *haatya pik'uunpa?*" Choate asked, then tore the meat from the bone. The answer didn't come easy for Cole. He filled his own mouth with food for time to ponder the last nine months.

In an attempt to clear his mind of the guilt left with the blood of a young Nez Percé woman on his hands, he took her eighteen-month-old daughter back to her native homeland. The long, cold journey across prairie and mountains cost the lives of others and nearly his own. Once at the end, the discovery that the native lands no longer held the infant's people led him to make the hardest and best choice.

Cole swallowed. "Yeah, I found them."

"The same you saw? The sheep people?"

"The same," Cole replied, tearing away more meat from the carcass. Silent Owl sat in the corner with the careful watch of a stray dog. It was then he realized it was her food he was eating. Even if she was an Indian woman and born into the custom of sacrifice for men, he didn't feel easy about it. However, it was Choate's home, and to surrender the food to her after it was offered to him would be the same insult as giving it to a stray dog.

"I gave the girl to them sheepers. The wife, she didn't take to the idea right off. I had to tell her about how I come across a baby. The mother in her took hold when I hung the kid from its heels, and she scampered out of that house and snatched the girl right from me." The joking manner Cole displayed brought a grin to Choate's face. Cole smiled, too, then remembered how a part of him went with that girl on that sheep farm. It was all he cared to recall. He had his fill of the roast as well. There was still enough for the squaw.

"I'm beholden to you for the food. Been a while since I've had a warm meal."

Choate nodded while picking his bird to bare bones. "You need it in you for the trip tomorrow."

Cole took a deep breath, leaned back in the chair, and clasped his knee with both hands. He had thought more than he wanted to about the decision to turn himself in to the army for court-martial during the trip from Idaho to Montana. He exhaled in a huff. "If it's the same with you, I'd rather set out today. The sooner the better."

"You need rest," said Choate. "Will take two weeks to get to Helena."

"I know. But I made up my mind near a year past. It ain't an easy thing to let sit. It ain't something I want rotting my head from the inside." Cole looked to the man he trusted to bring him in. "If I keep heading that way, it makes it easier to swallow. Keeps me from thinking, you know?"

He wasn't sure the bounty hunter truly understood. Moments passed as both men peered at each other. Just when Cole thought the message wasn't said in the right language, Choate nodded. "I get my gear."

The half-breed signaled to his woman, then went outside. By the way her eyes widened, Cole guessed she had just learned what they were planning. She rose like a soldier obeying orders and went to canvas

17

sacks in the corner. Flatbread cakes and dried jerky went from the many to two.

Cole left the shack for the corral. While he readied the palomino for the long ride, Choate saddled one of the ponies. "You sure you want leave today?"

"No," Cole replied and threw a stirrup on the seat to adjust the cinch. "But at least this way I ain't given myself a choice. Sounds loco, I know."

"No," Choate said. He led his horse to stand next to the palomino. "No, is not. Many time, chasing men to towns, territories, forests, mountains, I speak the same." They walked the horses to the front of the shack. Silent Owl stood on the porch holding two canvas sacks. Choate took them from her and kept talking. "When a man ask his soul should go on or go back," he said, walking to his horse to tie both sacks to the horn, "the man should go on 'til his soul tell him go back."

Cole mounted and saw Choate talk to the squaw with a mix of fists and fingers. Without a sign of fondness for the woman, he climbed into the saddle and nudged his roan. Cole kept the palomino still.

He peered directly into Silent Owl's eyes, and this time she didn't shy hers away. Not able to talk with his hands and sure she didn't know the white man's tongue enough to read his lips, he still felt obliged to thank her and tell her good-bye. However, her blank stare at him was hard to decipher. Did she know who he was and why her man was leaving? There wasn't a way for him to find the answer, and by her face it was as if she thought him an enemy. For a few moments, he kept his stare and simply raised his open palm. Then, heeding Choate's advice to move on, Cole nudged his palomino forward.

Jeff Tanner led five other riders up the hill. The late-summer morning provided a cool breeze. The good conditions would make the business at hand easier. The lack of heat kept sweat out of their eyes. The breeze would move the smoke from view.

He came upon the crest of the hill and reined in. Lee came along his side. Hix moved to the right outer flank with Morton. Clem and Harper took position on the left. Tanner did his best to act casual as the sentry pointed his Springfield.

"Stop right there."

Tanner raised his right hand. "Watch the aim of that rifle, Corporal. We're all friends here." He flashed a smile while glancing at his gang to make sure no one got edgy with

19

their pistols.

In a few moments, an officer rode up to their side. Tanner noticed three other soldiers prepare the wheel-mounted Gatling gun for targeting down the range.

"This is government property. State your business."

"Morning, Lieutenant. We ain't got no business to speak of. Me and the boys thought we would come up here and watch the show."

The officer cocked his head to the side and peered under the brim of his brown slouch hat. "And what show might that be?"

Tanner motioned ahead. "That a Gatling? Never seen one up close. Heard a lot about them, though. Rumor is it will fire a thousand rounds in a minute."

"Maximum fire is closer to twelve hundred if you could crank and load it that fast. But any rate of fire over six hundred makes for wild shots. Where are you men from?"

The question didn't surprise him, but he leaned back in the saddle for time to answer. "We are with the Point J Ranch. Out looking for strays when Lee here saw you boys setting up to fire. Thought it might be something to see."

The lieutenant eyed all six men in front of him. "That's quite a distance. The Point J is almost thirty miles south of here." He continued his stare to each of them, then centered on the leader. "Well, I'm sorry, Mr. . . ."

"Tanner."

"Mr. Tanner. This is federal land. We're not out here for public demonstration."

Tanner smiled more and nodded his head, then pointed ahead while draping his duster behind his holster. "That don't look like the same as in a picture I saw once. Appears to have more barrels than just six. And they look awful big for just a .32-caliber."

The officer didn't smile. "Ten barrels. And it's a .45-caliber. Mr. Tanner, I have to insist that you and your party leave immediately." He turned his head to the corporal. "Trooper, escort these men off the —"

The bullet piercing the lieutenant's back stopped his orders. Blood splashed the corporal's shirt as his commander fell face first to the ground. Shocked, he raised the rifle to his shoulder.

"Kill 'em!" Tanner yelled while recocking his pistol. All five drew their side arms and fired wildly. A bullet struck the corporal in the chest. Reflex pulled the Springfield's trigger. The loud shot whirred past Tanner's ear. Lee's head flew back and turned red the next instant. Tanner fired. Three more bullets were pumped into the soldier before he dropped the Springfield and collapsed.

The three other soldiers ran to their weapons. Tanner kicked his horse and charged while pulling back his pistol's hammer. Harper dove from his horse when the soldiers reached their rifles. The first got it to the shoulder before Tanner shot him in the head. Tanner fired again and another, but missed. The second soldier drew a bead on one of the riders. As he was about to fire, a slug exploded his neck. Blood fell like rain until the body hit the ground. Alone, the third tossed his rifle aside and ran down the far slope.

Tanner laughed as he watched the panicked escape. Harper stood, aimed his six-shooter, and fired. The trooper kept running. Clem picked up one of the Springfields and steadied it on the fleeing soldier.

"Wait," Tanner said as he dismounted.

Clem spoke through gritted teeth. "They killed Lee. We can't let none of them go. They'll tell the law and we'll have done this for nothing."

Tanner didn't return the stare or his anger. Casually he stepped behind the wheel-mounted Gatling gun. "Nobody said anything about letting him go." He turned his attention to the crates lying to the side of the wheels. A boot heel to the side sprang the shackle of the lock. The toe flung the lid open. Brass cartridges neatly lined the box, one stack atop another. "I always wanted to see what one of these could do." He pointed to the Bruce feeder. "Pick up that thing." Tanner scooped ten bullets and took the feeder from Clem. Slipping the cartridges down the feeder, he glimpsed the running soldier. He scooped ten more cartridges and fed them down the side. With both hands, he connected the feeder into the loading slot of the gun. "You'll have to spot me."

"I'd say he's a quarter mile by now."

Tanner swung the muzzles to the left in line with the target. A flick of the thumb raised the eye sight. He squinted, but fearing the aim was too low, he screwed the shim wheel left. Again, he squinted and saw his target through the sight. "Here goes."

He turned the crank. Three shots erupted with slight pressure. Awed by the power and temporarily blinded by the white cloud swirling around him, he leaned to the side to see. The soldier still ran down the slope.

"Where did they go?"

"About thirty yards shy of him," answered Harper. "Now he's running to the right. He knows you're shooting at him."

Tanner gradually swung the gun on the swivel and peered through the sight once more. He raised the level. "What you got to remember, it's just like shooting geese. If you don't lead them a little, you end up firing where they were rather than where they'll be at." Heeding his own advice, he pointed the muzzles in line with the soldier's stride. Once confident he had the line of fire, he turned the crank.

Rapid explosions sounded as one. Spent shells spilt like a waterfall to the ground. White smoke from the black powder drifted from view. Tanner kept cranking, the bullets pelting the slope and sending dirt popping in the air. Each shot closed the distance on the target, like a dog nipping at heels. A complete cycle of the crank exhausted the bullets in the feeder. The last three shots struck, blowing a hole in the man's chest and taking off one leg.

Tanner stood straight. He couldn't restrain the giddy laugh. "Damn. This is one fine piece of machinery!" He looked to Clem and Harper. They appeared stunned at the power of the weapon. "I told you." Tanner pointed at the cartridge crates. "Stack as many as you can on the carrier. Find them army mules and load them with the rest. We've got four hours to make seven miles."

CHAPTER TWO

The wagon crested the distant rise. Pulled by six draft horses and surrounded by the same count of armed riders, a single driver sat on top next to a shotgun-toting guard. The iron cell moved slowly, making for an easy target. A small barred window provided the only means to allow air inside. The design was solid, meant to keep intruders from breaking in and also keep the cargo from breaking out. It fit the plan perfectly.

Tanner put down the spyglass and scanned the hill to be sure the rest of the gang was out of sight. While he was prone on the ground, a peek above showed the leafy bushes gathered to hide the Gatling muzzles still in place. Again, he squinted through the eyehole to be certain the procession continued at a steady pace.

Once confident, he collapsed the spyglass and crawled back beyond the edge of the hill. He knelt next to an ammunition crate and drew the Bruce feeder, loading it by slipping the shells end first into the dual slots. The weapon had a capacity for twenty cartridges per slot; a pendulum kept the two rows apart, sliding open once the first slot emptied to allow a smooth transition for the next row of shells. He lifted the feeder atop the chamber slot and locked it in position.

He peeked through the leaves in front of the gun. Another fifty yards and the wagon would be at the spot on the road that the Gatling's aim had been set. Behind him, their horses and mules stood with reins tethered to the string between two trees. Once the firing started, they'd make a quick retrieval of the prize and a hasty escape. He turned his attention back to the side. Harper lay prone with an Army Springfield poised to fire. Morgan lay twenty feet farther. To the left, Clem took the same position, as did Hix. All was prepared.

Tanner stared down the sight. As the wagon neared the spot, he gripped the crank handle. Squinting one eye, he waited for the target to appear between the marks. Due to the slow pace of the team, it wasn't necessary to fire early. The lead pair entered into view, then the next pair. To steady his nerves, he slowly let out a breath, as if he were squeezing a trigger. The final pair of horses passed the view. The two men in the seat finally were in the sights.

Tanner rolled the crank forward. The barrels spun. After one full revolution came the initial burst of fire, sparks, and smoke. "Open fire!" he yelled, the white cloud in front of him obscuring his target. He stopped the crank to allow the smoke to drift. When he again saw the wagon, only the lead pair of horses were on their feet, straining to run, but unable to budge the deadweight and wagon behind them. The bloody bodies of the driver and shotgun guard slumped atop the iron box. The riders scattered for cover behind the wagon. Two fell out of the saddle from the rifle fire.

His own nerves jumping, his breath short with excitement, Tanner let out a hoot and resumed cranking. The barrels spun, firing the hail storm of lead. Bullets ricocheted off the iron box. One of the armed riders dove from his mount and leaned against the end of the wagon, raising his rifle. Tanner swung the Gatling in line at the guard. Shots pierced the shoulder, neck, and head.

The explosions ceased. Despite continued cranking, all the rounds in the feeder were gone. Finally, Tanner stopped. With a glance to the right and left he saw the gang give him a stare, first one of fright, then easing into a gleeful smile. Tanner smacked the hot breech. Below lay the corpses of eight men who were alive and healthy just thirty seconds before. "Let's get down there and get him out."

Tanner went to his horse and mounted, the energy from the crank handle still buzzing in his hands. He rode down the slope and came upon the wagon. Blood poured from the wounds of the dead men. As he came next to the iron cell, he saw that stray shots had dented the metal but had not penetrated.

He slowed his horse and reined in at the rear of the wagon. A padlock sealed the double doors. Tanner removed his revolver and took aim at the shackle. He fired twice, the second shot splitting the shackle. He dismounted and threw the shattered lock from the doors.

Slowly he swung open the first door, then the other. Inside was the reason for the attack. In a black-striped dirty white shirt and rough gray pants sat the short figure with hair cut a half inch above the scalp.

"You son of a bitch," he said. "You nearly killed me with that thing. Three of them shots came through the window." He rose to a crouch and walked out of the wagon. The two men stood beside each other, staring at the man in front of them. The prisoner looked to the dead guard on the ground. "Looks like it worked." A bright grin cracked his face. Tanner and he hugged in a brotherly embrace.

"Don't appear too bad, Coy."

"Look at you. Blond hair running over your ears, and with that hat brim pulled to the sides, people around here will swear they seen Custer's ghost. Looks like you're eating better than me, too. I haven't ate a decent cooked meal in a month." He looked to the ridge, and Tanner followed his eyes. "That Clem and Harper?"

The riders slowly led the dual mule team pulling the Gatling gun down the hill. "Yeah, and Howard Morgan and Jim Hixson from the Hatley bunch. I told them there was more money in what we got planned."

Coy smiled but continued to scan the ridge. "Where's Lee?"

Tanner let his smile fade. "Dead. He took a bullet when we stole that crank gun."

Coy's jowl sank. "You got him killed?" He backhanded Tanner. "I told you not to lose a man chasing that thing."

Tanner rubbed the sting from his cheek. "If I didn't, those guards would still be alive and we'd be stuck up on that ridge. If I hadn't killed them quick, how long it be before they'd turn their guns on you?" He stopped rubbing when his point turned the short man to his side. "Can't expect to charge a trooper detail and not take some lead back. I wasn't trying to get him killed. But he got shot."

The explanation didn't brighten Coy's attitude. The short man took a lamented breath. "Let's get the hell out of here and on to the business planned."

After a night's sleep, Cole's mood was a bit more chipper. The long weeks in the saddle had put him in a stupor. Once they made camp, all he wanted was some uninterrupted rest without having to keep one eye half open. It was a comfort to have Choate watch his back.

During the morning ride, the two hadn't spoken more than three words. Not one to give too much meaning to matters buried deep in the gut, he cast a glimpse or two at the half-breed with whom he shared this trail. The two shared more than that.

A colored man named Jenks acted as a father for Cole when he left the troopers twelve years before. The Army scout took in the kid and taught him life's ways when in the wilderness. Cole relied on those lessons many times to save himself from starvation and ambush. It was only while riding the plains to slaughter buffalo that both men learned the past of the other. Jenks told the stories of traveling through the world of white men and natives. Among those came the tale of taking a Crow bride for the cost of his best saddle ponies. A winter later, he planted a baby in the squaw's belly. Jenks took her back to her tribe for the child to be raised by her own people, leaving only a name of the Frenchman who once saved his own life for his son to bear.

Threading their way through the passes where mountains still topped with snow took up more than half the sky, Cole steered the palomino close behind Choate's lead between the trees. Although many miles were still ahead of them, if something was to be said, it may take every inch of the trip for it to all come out.

"Hey, Choate," he said, only sparking a slight glance behind. "Where's this place we're headed?"

"Copper Springs. Mine town."

"And you know the law there, you said?"

It took a moment before there was a decipherable nod. "Sheriff. He a good man. We sleep in his jail. Maybe food." He shrugged. "Maybe not."

31

The notion that they would end up in a jail in order to have a roof overhead with the slight chance of a hot meal brought a snicker to Cole. "Sounds like your old man. Now, there was a man could get what he needed no matter what."

Choate didn't answer.

The path widened only slightly, but it was enough for Cole to edge the palomino to come alongside. There was something gnawing at his insides that needed to be relieved. "You know, I was the last one that saw him."

The remark hung in the breeze for more than a minute before Choate barely turned his head. "Ain't my business."

Cole cocked his head to the side. "Well, I can understand the feeling. He wasn't much of what you call a father. But he did talk about you." He dipped his head to the ground while the horses walked straight. "He was proud to have a boy. May not to have said in just that way, but he was proud you were his son."

Choate kept his eyes front. "Him? My mother died because of him. Because of me."

"Can't say nothing about that except I'm sorry to learn of her passing." He took a deep breath. "I guess what I'm getting at, I think I knew him as you were meant to. I mean, as a man should know his pa." The words came as easy as ramming his hand down his throat to rip solid lead from the pit of his stomach. "I know we ain't no blood kin. But I guess we have something from the same man. You got his blood in your bones." His eyes rolled to the blue sky. "I got his teaching. Sometimes it was preaching, but it was what got me this far." He let out a huff. "There, I said my piece."

With only a minor weight gone from his insides, Cole aimed his eyes straight as Choate had. The path narrowed. He slowed the palomino in order to ride behind in single file.

CHAPTER THREE

On a far green hill two tall stacks billowed smoke to the north high into the sky. Passing through the opium dens and brothels hidden inside tattered tents, Cole and Choate rode side by side into the center of town. Cole noticed the fresh wood of the buildings, pillars, and boardwalks. Mostly men walked the muddy streets with their pant legs tucked inside their boots. Occasionally, a woman wearing an apron poked her head from the upper windows to hang laundry. Other women scrubbing clothes in buckets in the alleys appeared to be the only white females in the town. A harsh metal smell hung in the air. Cole turned to Choate and wrinkled his nose.

"Copper," Choate said. The bounty hunter pointed to the twin stacks. "The mine."

When they steered into a street to the left, numerous shops with large letters painted in slanted lines and circles on the windows and glass doors sat butted next to one another. A growler boy crossed the street with pails of beer hanging from a long stick propped on his shoulder.

In the center of the stretch of buildings stood a double-story opera house. Four columns as thick as any aged oak trunk and carved to resemble growing vines supported the considerable awning over the wide steps leading from the street to the double doors. Next to the doors, a life-sized poster of a woman was displayed behind a pane of glass.

A small building stood separate from the rest. Its brick walls and barred windows and door left little doubt of its business. Cole had come this far. Now came the time for him to hold true to the nagging voice in his head telling him this was right.

Choate dismounted and reined to the hitch post. Cole followed suit. They stepped on the boardwalk. Out of the door came a short older man with a tin star, a gray short-brimmed hat, a checkered shirt, and a paunch putting a strain on his belt. Tucked in the belt was a short barrel revolver.

"Well, fancy seeing you," he said with a squeak to his voice. "You two chasing after Coy Dallas too, I see." Choate first looked at Cole, then shook his head. "You're not?

Haven't you heard? Dallas broke from a prison wagon yesterday. Marshals were taking him to Deer Lodge, and the rumor is his gang ambushed them on the road about thirty miles from here. Killed the guards, and it's said all of them is headed north. Figured bounty hunters like you fellas would be quick to pick up his scent."

Again Choate shook his head, then pointed at Cole. "I bring him in."

The short lawman appeared confused. He pointed also. "Him? Who's he?"

"Name Clay Cole," said Choate as the lawman eyed Cole from the dust-colored boots to the black hat. Once at the top, those eyes drifted down and locked at the single-action Colt snugged in the right hip holster. Choate continued. "Going to Helena. I told we stay here for night to rest horses and get food. I say I know you. I trust you."

The lawman shook his head. "Let me get this right," he said, wagging his finger at both of them. "You're bringing him in? He's an outlaw? Wanted? And you let him ride in here wearing that hogleg?" He finished by directing the finger at the pistol.

Cole lifted the Colt from the holster, to the wide-eyed surprise of the lawman. Then, twisting it butt first with the barrel in his palm, Cole surrendered it.

"I can't say I ever had a man with papers on him ever hand over his weapon so plainly." The lawman offered his hand. "Hap Stillman, Cantrell County Sheriff. Welcome to Copper Springs, Montana."

"Clay Cole. Good to be here, I think."

"Pleased to meet you, Mr. Cole."

"Call me Clay. Choate said he trusts you. I'm willing to, so I stay alive in this place."

"Well, come on in." Stillman opened the door and tossed the Colt on a desk. "Come to think of it, I may have heard that name." He turned around as Cole and Choate entered. "There was a man named Cole who was in Idaho near three months back, maybe longer. Killed a rancher name of Cauley. Heb Cauley. Most of his gunny hands, too. There was no charges. Folks there I heard said it was self-defense." His eyes again measured Cole. "Some said it was the Rainmaker. The one with Custer." Stillman's stiff stare appeared as if he stood in a trance.

"Same man," Choate said as he walked farther inside.

The sheriff's brushy mustache slowly parted like a pair of drapes, revealing a gleam usually showed at proud occasions. "I don't believe it. You're him? The Rainmaker? The one it's said rode with Custer? Survived the slaughter to seek out the savages all alone that done it. The same one said to have killed fifty men by himself?" Again, Stillman shoved his open hand to Cole.

Not comfortable with stretching the truth, Cole thought it best to explain as little as needed. With the mood his host was in, the tactic might mean better food. He shook Stillman's hand once more. "I never kept count."

"I am very pleased to meet you, sir. Not often — in fact, never — had a man of your stature in our midst. Anything I can do for you, it'd be an honor to do so."

Confused by the generosity, Cole cast an eye at Choate, who kept a stern face. Not wanting to ruin the good spirits, he forced a smile. "Glad I could oblige."

"Yes, sir, I'm glad you're here. What can I get you?"

"Been in a saddle for all but a few hours for the last three months. Wouldn't mind something a little softer."

"Can't blame you a bit. Know the feeling myself, only now can't stand to ride more than an hour. Rheumatism pains me something awful." Stillman fumbled with keys taken from a hook on the wall while retreating back into the jail hall. Two cells in the corner angled from each other. Stillman opened the door on the one at the right. "Just got this one cleaned."

Slowly, Cole walked through the barred threshold. A mattress full of clumps lay atop a wooden bunk built out from the wall. A large bucket half filled with sand sat in the corner. A quick glance showed the only other thing in the cell was him. He faced Stillman.

"I hope you'll be at home in there. I know it ain't much. All I have for the time being." Cole nodded. The sheriff pointed at Cole's gunbelt. "I guess I should ask for that. The knife, too. If you don't mind. It wouldn't look right if I was to keep a man in here with something like that."

Cole slipped the hank knot from his thigh and popped the leather strap from the buckle. He slid the sheath holding the wood-handled Bowie knife from the belt and handed all the belongings to Stillman.

"Ought to give me your hat, too. No place to hang it in there. Wouldn't want it to get hurt on the floor."

Cole removed the wide-brimmed hat and passed it along as well. "Anything else? Need my drawers, too?"

Stillman laughed. "No, sir. I'll bring you a

bucket of water and a rag so you can wash up if you like." The sheriff shut the cell door and turned the latch. "I'll bring you some dinner, too. I know you must be hungry. And take your horse to the livery and have the saddle and the rest brought here for safekeeping. Can't wait to tell all that we have a famous man in the flesh in our jail." Still shaking his head, he went to the outer door.

Amused by the sheriff's delight, Cole sat on the mattress and groaned at the ache in his back. Choate stood in the same place for the entire time. "Where you sleeping?"

The big dark man, still with a firm jowl, stepped to the cell door. "Coy Dallas. Big reward coming."

"Who is he?"

"Thief. Rustler. Mankiller."

The simple description said more than the few words. "Know anything about him?"

Choate shook his head. "Rides good. Going to north. Try to hide. Wait for law to follow. Kill them as they come."

"Sure you want to go alone?" asked Cole. He didn't often offer to involve himself in matters not directly related to his own skin. However, Choate was like family and could use his help.

Choate looked around the cell and then at

Cole while slightly shaking his head. "Caught you alone."

The remark brought a snicker. "All right, you black fool," said Cole as Choate wandered to the door. "I'll be thinking of you out there in the brush while I'm in here under a roof, dry, by that hot stove in the night, eating food cooked by someone knows how, free of pests crawling on my skin." He stopped as the bounty hunter gripped the doorknob to leave the jail. "Choate." The big bounty hunter paused. They faced each other eye-to-eye for a brief instant. "Keep your head down."

CHAPTER FOUR

The call of a bird brought Cole out of his sleep. As he sat up, he followed the song to peer outside the bars to the office window at the top of the wall. The natural sound forced a deep sigh. He no longer had the same freedom the bird enjoyed.

His back against the wall of his cell, he pondered his decision for an hour just as he had on the long ride from Idaho, the same question that burdened him for the last six months. Since deciding in Texas to come north and confront the charges against him, the possibility of not being believed and serving the rest of his life in chains or facing a firing squad ate away at his gut.

For near seven years he avoided the decision. It put him on the run to a life of constantly looking over his shoulder. Blistering days in the saddle, cold nights on the ground, spoiled food, and water from mudholes persuaded him more than any words.

However, solitude pained him more than any of the elements.

He always shied his face from prying eyes. Any mention of the Seventh or Little Bighorn would chase him faster than a grizzly off a fresh kill. Never could he take safe haven in the company of law-abiding folk without fear of being discovered. It was the price he paid to be able to ride anywhere he wished, at any time, just the same as that bird outside.

The rattle of the front doorknob got his attention. Sheriff Stillman unlocked the latch, pushed the door open, then slowly bent to lift the cloth-covered tray from the boardwalk. He stepped into the office and kicked the door closed. "Good morning to you."

"Same to you," Cole answered. The smell of warm bread wafted his way. "Ain't polite to eat in front of those that ain't got nothing to eat."

"Oh, don't worry about me." Stillman took the cell keys off the hook and unlocked the cell door. "I already ate."

Confused, Cole watched as the old lawman retrieved the tray and brought it into the cell. It took a moment before Cole accepted it. "For me?"

"Why, of course. Wouldn't be proper not

to feed a guest, even if he is a prisoner." The aroma had Cole pull away the cloth to reveal fresh eggs, warm biscuits, and three strips of crisp bacon. He steadied the appetizing breakfast on his lap and didn't know what to say.

"I'll have coffee at a boil in just a few minutes," Stillman said as he left the cell and locked the door.

Still amazed, Cole tucked the napkin into his collar and picked up the metal fork. "Much obliged for the food. Not often I get a real breakfast. Pass it on to your Mrs." He stabbed the eggs with the fork.

"Oh, I'm a widower."

Feeling a fool, Cole mumbled, "Sorry. Didn't mean no offense."

Stillman threw a match into the stove. "None taken," he said without a hint of sorrow. "Lost my Martha nearly four years ago." He put the pot atop the iron plate. "No. That was courtesy of Mrs. Amy Courtwright. She stopped me just before I came here. Said she wanted to see that you were fed proper as a guest in our town. I promised she could come in here and take a peek at you."

Cole stopped chewing and glanced at the door.

"Oh, she ain't coming right now. She

wanted to put on her best to be seen by a famous man. You know how women are. Can't be seen as they are every day." Cole took another bite of the eggs and snapped a bacon strip in half. Stillman sat in his chair. "Truth be, I've had quite a few folks needle at me for a peek at you. Seems word has spread pretty fast about you being here."

The idea perplexed Cole. "For what?"

"Hellfire man, you're the Rainmaker. The last white man to see Custer alive. Ain't many can claim that they will see you in the flesh. Be a big boast to neighbors and kin to claim to lay eyes on you."

Not understanding the attraction, Cole didn't let it stop his meal. He finished both bacon strips and scooped the eggs in his mouth with a few strokes of the fork. He picked up a biscuit to discover melted butter soaking the inside. He bit into it. The bread was as tasty as rare beef. The hospitality was a pleasant surprise. At no time in his life was he ever as welcome in a place as he'd been in this one. The reason didn't appear plain, but if it meant meals as good as this breakfast, he wasn't one to refuse a few more visitors.

A knock at the door turned his and the sheriff's attention to the door. After slowly rising from the chair, Stillman went to the door and opened. Murmured voices were too low to understand, so Cole finished the biscuit and took a bite from the other. In a few minutes, Stillman left the door ajar and came to the cell.

"There's a young fellow out there. Says he's a reporter for a newspaper back east and would like to have a word with you. I told him that you were enjoying breakfast, and since I didn't know him, I don't want to ask you on account of him."

The request didn't seem a threat. "What's he want to know?"

Stillman shrugged. "I guess what everyone else wants to know. Just to have a talk with you. I can tell him no. Won't make me no difference."

Cole shook his head. "I don't 'spect that would cause me any trouble. Not in here, at least. Bring him in."

Stillman shrugged again, then went to the door and escorted the young man to the cell. He wore a dark tweed coat, a cloth vest over a stiff white shirt, and a wide silver tie at the collar. Brown trousers wrapped around his slim waist and covered the tops of his leather shoes. He removed the gray bowler in respect. "Mr. Cole, my name is Richard Johnson. I'm with *Harper's Weekly* of New York City. I'd like to ask you a few questions, if you don't mind."

Cole paused a moment as he finished chewing, then stuck the rest of the biscuit in his mouth and mumbled. "Have at it."

The young man drew a paper pad from the right coat pocket and a pencil from the left. "Thank you. First, when were you born? And where?"

The question riled him. "Why you want to know?"

"Oh," the reporter said with the apologetic face of a child, "just general interest. Our readers want to know. They find it helps them to know the person they're reading about."

The explanation didn't settle his mind. "Ain't got nothing to do with what I done."

"Oh, I know. Tell you what, let's go on." The kid's blue eyes focusing on the paper reminded him of his own. He stared at the smooth face, which showed only a few shaved stubbles. Sympathy got the best of him.

"Twenty-six of September. Eighteen and fifty. Fort Scott, Kansas."

The reporter's head popped up at the answer. He let loose with a grateful smile. "And was your father a soldier?"

Cole nodded. "A captain. Served in the Missouri Sixty-second in the war."

The reporter scribbled on the pad, keeping his eyes on the paper. "Are they still alive?"

"What?" Cole heard the question. He didn't like it.

Again, in a remorseful tone, the question was asked. "Is either of your parents still with us?"

"Son," he huffed, "my ma died of the consumption back in 'sixty-one. My pa was killed in Texas during the last battle of the war, a month after Lee surrendered. Why that is of interest to the people reading your paper I cannot figure. If you got more questions about them, better leave now, or forget about asking."

The kid's eyes widened. "Yes sir. I mean, no sir. I won't ask any more questions about them. I'm sorry if I offended."

Cole let his mood simmer. He wished he had another biscuit. The time savoring them could be used to consider any more answers. "Tell me — what's your name again?"

"Richard, sir. Richard Johnson."

"Well, Richard, why are you here asking me these questions?"

The reporter seemed surprised at the question. "Why, you're the Rainmaker."

More of a brand than a name, it was given to him by his mother the day he was born.

It now served as hound, howling at his presence and nipping at his heels. Cole shrugged a single shoulder. "Some people call me that."

Richard looked to Stillman, who slowly scooted the soles of his boots across the wooden floor so as to not spill a drop from the coffee tin he slipped through the bars. Cole accepted the hot cup and slurped the steaming brew. He winked his approval for the strong taste.

Richard looked to his pad. "So is it true that you are the man that was with Colonel Custer? If I remember correctly, you are sought by the Army in regard to the massacre. Am I correct?"

Cole slowly swallowed. The burn of the coffee was small compared to the fire burning in his gut. It was the question that haunted him to this very day. It was the reason for his return. He wasn't of a mind to confess to this young kid.

"If that's what you came to ask, you come a long way for nothing." Cole faced about to return to the bunk. Another question stopped him.

"Legend has it you rode with Wild Bill Hickok?"

"It's true. But he's dead. Seen the grave myself in Deadwood."

"Exactly," said Richard, pointing a finger. "Shot in the back. As was Jesse James just two months ago in Missouri." The news raised Cole's brow. "Yes, it's true. He was shot for reward money by one of his own gang. And so is Billy the Kid. He was killed in New Mexico by Sheriff Pat Garrett."

The names sounded familiar. "Billy the Kid? He a odd-looking fella with a bovine jaw?"

Richard shook his head. "I can't say. I never met him, nor saw a true picture of him."

Cole looked to Stillman. "Seems I met up with a peculiar kid in Texas that some bounty hunters were after. May not have been him. But he did seem more than a mite touched in the head."

"I believe he had that reputation," said Stillman.

"Yes," Richard continued. "Don't you see? You're the last. You are the last of the legendary figures of the Western frontier."

Although the kid's tone of voice was bright, Cole didn't like the company he penned him with. "Are you trying to say I'm a bank robber?"

Once more came the childlike denial. "No. No. Not what I'm saying at all." Richard cleared his throat. "In the East, there is an entire population who do not know what life is like beyond the Mississippi River. They don't understand the ideal of an open prairie, where a man can ride for days on end without coming across another man. Where wild savages live in the same manner they have for centuries. They don't know what it's like to hunt a buffalo or other exotic animals just to have something to eat. In a way, you might say they live the same adventure through the pages of books." He stared at Cole like a small boy eyeing a father. "You are the type of man they want to live these adventures through. When they read them, they want to think of you." Cole cast an eye at Stillman, who held a look of concern.

"See here, young fellow," said the sheriff. "The West has changed since them days. This is eighteen-eighty-two. We got plenty of folks living out here in Montana. Heck, Copper Springs itself is the second-largest town in the territory. There's over ten thousand people living within a hundred miles of here. We got a newspaper, three churches, an opera house, and fifteen barbers. Heckfire, John L. Sullivan himself is coming here two months from now to take on all comers."

"Who?" Cole asked, unsure of the name.

"He is a boxer," Richard answered. When Cole raised a brow of ignorance, the reporter continued. "He fights people for money. Often he comes to mining camps like this —"

"Town. Mining town," Stillman angrily corrected.

"Town, excuse me. He'll come here to challenge anyone to stay in the ring with him for three minutes. He also fights other professional boxers, for prize money. Sullivan is considered the world champion now."

"I know of the practice. Never heard of no world champion. So he fights all in the crowd until they admit he's the best in the world?"

Richard cracked a smile and shook his head. "No."

Cole raised his brow and cocked his head to the side. The idea bewildered him. "Must be good money in it. One thing for a man to like to fight; it's another to get paid for it enough to travel about the world."

The young reporter shook his head again. "Let's go on to something else. Who was the first man you killed?"

Cole's chest tightened, his heart beat faster, and his brow drew down. He glanced to Stillman, who appeared just as surprised by the inquiry. "You think I take pride in knowing. Like I got it scratched on paper or make it a memory?"

Richard cracked a grin, but it faded quickly once he noticed that Cole kept his scowl. "Well, I, uh, I didn't mean any harm by it. It's just that some men that I have read about, uh, famous shootists of the West, can recall with great detail about those they've shot."

Cole peered into the young reporter's eyes. "Listen, son. When you pump a slug in a man, watch him all squeezed with pain, blood pouring out of him and into the dirt, and you did it 'cause you didn't want a slug pumped into you, it ain't a proper matter of asking him while watching him die what his name was, and repeating it so to commit it to memory. As a fact, it's something I've never been anxious to recall." He slurped hot coffee so to cool his temper. "Who are these famous 'shootists' you heard of that make it a practice on bragging who they killed?"

Richard cleared his throat. "Well, just recently I read how Wyatt Earp described a gunfight he engaged in with his brothers against a band of cowboys in Arizona last October."

"I read about that myself, a copy of the *Tombstone Epitaph*," said Stillman. "The

53

copy was passed to me and said eight men were all shooting at less than ten feet of each other."

"Earp?" Cole said, reminded of the name. "A fellow name Earp was the law in Dodge City, Kansas."

Stillman nodded. "It's the same one. He got run out of Dodge and went to Arizona to mine and run the faro game in a saloon there. Or so said the paper."

All attention turned to a knock at the door. Stillman hurried to open it. "Come on in, Mrs. Courtwright."

He escorted the plain woman to the center of the office, trailed by a boy of near ten years old who removed his hat once inside. As the woman came closer to the cell, Cole could see that under her brown shawl the long white dress had wide blue stripes from the lace collar down to the hem.

Stillman continued. "This is the kind lady that cooked your breakfast, Clay."

Cole smiled the best he could at the unattractive woman. "I'm beholden for your thoughtfulness, Mrs. Courtwright."

She smiled with a slight blush, then drew the boy in front of her. "I brought my son. This is Thomas. He wanted to see you. Thomas, say hello to Mr. Cole."

"Hello," the shy boy greeted with a wave.

Normally not of a mind to put on a show for folks, Cole remembered another kid of the same age back in New Mexico. The memory forced him to take a knee and extend his hand through the bars. "Good to meet you, Thomas."

"This will make a great photograph," Richard said. He rose from the chair and headed for the door. "I'll be back in a moment with my camera. Don't move." As he opened the door, a line of townsfolk stood waiting to enter the office. While Thomas hesitated to accept Cole's hand, the citizens strolled into the office, one after another, gawking and muttering to one another. Cole cast an eye at Stillman.

The lawman shrugged. "Folks are naturally curious."

Not comfortable with their stares, Cole began to rise to retreat to the bunk. The action brought Thomas closer, perhaps in fear of losing the chance to shake the hand of a famous shootist. Cole knelt again and took the kid's hand. Not a word was said, but the effort was rewarded when the kid turned to smile at his mother.

Just as the mutterings of the crowd crested, they receded. The hush drew Cole's attention to the door. The people parted, revealing a taller-than-normal woman wearing a fancy dark gown reflecting shades of purple and green. The small hat pinned atop her bundled red hair held the same pattern. The purse matched as well, and wasn't big enough to store much more than a stick of gum.

The men removed their hats as she walked to the center of the room. Mrs. Courtwright held Thomas close to her skirt like there was some fear. This respect wasn't commonly shown to a parlor woman. Cole glanced at Stillman, who also had his hat in hand. Unsure of the identity of the woman, Cole retreated to sit on the bunk.

With all eyes fixed to her, the tall redhead issued a polite smile, but not one of genuine delight. In little time, the wives who had brought their men to the jail didn't appear comfortable with this woman around their husbands. Just as they entered, each couple, including Mrs. Courtwright and Thomas, filed out of the office, leaving the lady alone in the center of the room. The smile gone, she stood, just staring at Cole without uttering a sound, like she was pondering the purchase of a horse. As she stared at him, he took careful notice of her.

Her fair complexion was as smooth as a sheet of new paper, serving as proper parchment for her apple-red lips, shaded pink cheekbones, and sky-blue eyes. Long strands of shiny beads hung from each ear. Similar beads were linked around her slim neck, and a large jade gem stretched down to the gown, which had no collar. The top of her chest wasn't quite as white as her face. Her bust wasn't the biggest he'd seen, but the squared bodice fit tight enough to squeeze the hint of a cleft.

She glanced at Stillman, who still stood at attention like a dutiful private to an officer. She flashed that polite smile for only a second, then turned for the open door. Without looking back, she walked out of the office. The back of the dress conformed to her natural hips without the padding of a bustle.

Cole continued looking at the vacant threshold. "Who is she?"

The lawman let out a long-held breath. "That was Miss Vivien Hooper," he said with the tone of a revelation.

Cole faced Stillman. "She own this town or something?"

The sheriff put his hat back on and cracked a smile. "She could if she wanted to. She's a singer. A voice like a bird. Came here from Helena. She puts on one hell of a show, I'll tell you. I heard she has sung on a stage in San Francisco." His eyes locked in wonder and he muttered in a hollow tone, "One of the prettiest gals I have ever seen here." He broke from his daydream and eyed Cole. "That's the first time I've seen her outside of the opera house. She sure must have been taken with you to come in here. I heard she's as shy as a possum in the daylight."

"With me? I never heard of her. How would she know me?"

"Like I said. Folks are naturally curious."

Footsteps pounded the wooden boardwalk. Richard came through the open door with a large box mounted on three aligned sticks slung on his shoulder. After one step into the office, he stopped and held a puzzled face. "Where did everyone go?"

"You missed the show, son." Stillman poured himself another tin full of coffee. "They all left once Vivien Hooper stopped by."

"Vivien Hooper was here? The opera star?"

"The same. Was here not more than a minute ago. But she's gone now. Likely won't see here again before she boards the stage tomorrow."

"She leaving?" Cole asked.

Stillman nodded. "She's been in town for two weeks. Would have been gone today

58

had the Wells Fargo not been caught in the high water of Kingman Valley from the thaw's runoff. But I had word from the telegraph that they are on their way. Seems a shame she couldn't put on one more show." He winked at Cole. "I know you'd like it."

Richard's shoulders slumped, then he shrugged. "Well, since I'm here with the camera, I might as well get a photograph of you."

Cole lay on the bunk. "Not in a mood for one." He closed his eyes. Sleep wasn't something he'd caught enough of over the last six months. Now, with a roof over his head and behind a locked door, he afforded himself the pleasure.

Choate cautiously approached the iron wagon. The stench of death hung in the mild breeze. Buzzards pecked at the hide of the dead horses. The blood from the large wounds had dried into the dirt, having not been washed into the soil by any rain. Other dried pools outlined where the men fell. Their bodies already were claimed by family. No one bothered to bury the animals or burn the carcasses. They left the task to nature to dispose of them.

He dismounted and went to the wagon.

The metal plates on the sides held dents but no holes. He ran his fingers over the marks, feeling the angle of indentation, then turned and looked at the ridge over his left shoulder. A few more steps and he stood in front of the double doors. After another cautious scan to the left and right, he stepped inside. The air was heavy. The single window made for little air to flow through the iron jail. Before he left the interior, more scrapes marked the walls. There was no blood on the floor. He looked to the window once more and peered between the three bars. In the line of sight was the distant ridge.

Choate left the wagon and went to his horse. While riding to the top of the ridge, he noticed one set of hoofprints. As he approached the summit, more riders' tracks were easily noticeable. He counted at least four. Two other prints were of unshod animals. Possibly those of mules.

Shiny brass cartridge casings drew his attention. He slid off the saddle and picked up one from the pile of dozens. The diameter appeared to be .44 or .45 caliber, but the length of the shell wasn't common. The powder was still fresh. As he contemplated what type of rifle could fire the long shell, he saw a pair of ruts trailing down the side of the ridge.

The jangle of keys woke Cole. He raised one sleepy eyelid. The sheriff fumbled with the latch in the dim light. He wiped his other eye and sat up on the bunk as Stillman opened the cell door. "What are you doing?"

Without his usual friendly tone, the lawman answered. "I'm taking you out of here." He motioned for Cole to follow him to his desk. Cole glanced at the window, where the light outside barely illuminated the office. He rose off the bunk and went to the desk. Although the rest was the best he had enjoyed in some time, he didn't think he slept through the night. "What time of day is it?"

"Near eight o'clock." Stillman opened a drawer and removed a pair of shackles. "Hate to have to do this. But it wouldn't be proper to have you seen out there without wearing these. Hold out your hands, Clay."

He complied. During the short time in the jail, he had thought himself safe for the first time in three years. As the lawman wrapped the irons around each wrist, his heart sank. He glanced at the door, not knowing what waited for him outside. It made sense why none of the lamps in the room were lit. Easier to ride him out of town with the cover of dark.

"What are you doing?"

"What I've been paid to do."

"Where we going?"

"I can't say I'm proud of what I'm doing. I think the less said about it the better."

"Someone pay you to give me up?" Cole asked as he was paraded for the door. His mind still not clear with the sleep, the notion of putting up a fight came late now that he was wearing iron. He couldn't shoot a pistol with his hands chained together. "Bill Wheeler out there? A bounty hunter with a limp? He the one paying you?"

Stillman opened the door. "I ain't sure what's planned for you. But it ain't nobody by that name. Come on, let's go." He led Cole out of the office, off the boardwalk, and into the street. Dusk made it hard to see far, but a few folks walked beneath the gleaming street lanterns a few hundred feet away. He thought to yell, but who would help a prisoner escape from the local law? Stillman peered in that direction while holding the chain to keep it from rattling. He paused with the sound of a voice in the dark, but once it passed, he proceeded across the street.

Cole's chest was tight. He scanned to the left and right, waiting for riders to approach. If he was to be taken from town, that was the quickest way. Once they were on the far boardwalk, he heard music through the wooden walls of a building. He went into a pitch-black alley between the two buildings. The music grew louder. Unable to see, he was ready to break and run at the first sight or sound of a gun drawn or a hammer cocked. All he heard was the music as Stillman paraded him farther into the dark.

All at once, he stopped and bumped into the lawman's back. "Sorry," whispered the sheriff. Cole was turned right and stumbled against a wood step. Thinking it another boardwalk, he climbed the step to discover there was another. Cautiously, he continued up stairs, but after only three, there were no more.

"I don't know about you, Clay. But twenty dollars is a lot of money. Especially if it all shows up in my pocket at once." Another jangle of a key could be heard, and there was more fumbling with a latch. "I only get paid thirty-five dollars a month." Bright light shined into Cole's eyes. A door had been opened and the music crashed into his ears. He now stood on a three-step landing in front of a side door to a building. "The offer was just too good to pass up." Stillman led the way inside and closed the door behind them. Light came from farther inside the building, as did the music, which now came with a voice singing. A woman's voice.

The two of them crept slowly farther inside. Cole glanced about, noticing the black-draped surroundings. They edged closer to a narrow opening of tall red curtains. In the next two steps, he recognized he was on a stage, hidden from the view of a large crowd of men sitting in a theater. On the stage, with a dozen lanterns beaming at her, pranced the red-haired woman he'd seen in the jail, only now all she wore was a black and red corset and black stockings hooked by garters up to her thighs. She stretched out a long high note and turned her head toward him. Stillman tossed her the key to the shackles. She caught it without missing a word to the tune, winked once, and tucked it into her bosom while still holding the high note.

Stillman grunted his throat clear. "You have a good evening, Clay." The lawman left Cole's side with a wry grin, then went out the side door. Able to take a breath again, Cole turned his attention back to the gal on the stage. Unsure of what was planned for him, he tried to relieve his mind of worry and enjoy the show.

As darkness closed in, Choate followed the dim light to the west. More than once, he'd had to slide off the saddle to find the trail of tracks. He had traveled at least five miles since the ruts split with another pair of tracks from the two he now followed.

Through brush, he bobbed his head from side to side to find broken limbs or bent stems of wild grass. The steady trail of hoof marks on the ground came to a stop. Boot heels were pressed in the dirt. He peered at his surroundings, but all appeared as it had for the last mile or more of scattered brush and tall grass. Slowly, he slid off the saddle and drew his Winchester.

He pulled back the rifle hammer and cautiously stepped around a bend in the thick bushes. In the center of a clearing stood a homestead. He couldn't make out if it was built of wood or sod, so he crept closer. On the far side, tall branches of a tree stood beyond the height of the roof. With each slow step he neared the house. The light sank with the setting sun. He followed the footprints on his knees, so as not to waste the last minutes of visibility.

He came upon the side of the house.

Quickly, he put his back to the outer wall. His fingers sensed wood. A low-tone creak, like that of rope or twine under a strain, broke the silence. He paused to determine the direction of the sound. Turning to his right, he crept slowly to the back of the house.

Unsure of the source, he took off his hat so the brim wouldn't poke around the corner sooner than he wanted. Putting his right cheek against the wood wall, he edged his left eye beyond the wall, ready to shoot at the first movement. The silhouette of a body swung by the neck from a tree against the barely lit western sky.

Choate came full around the corner, reaching for the knife from his belt. He put down the rifle and reached for the legs to spare the weight on the rope. As he grabbed the boots, hard metal crashed against his skull. His face in the dust and grass, the throbbing pounded into his brain. Despite the pain, he heard men laugh.

"It's a nig. Probably looking to rob the place," a giddy voice spoke. The click of a gun hammer crackled through the air, but the tingle running through Choate's body kept him from scrambling after the Winchester. "Sorry, fella. Looks like we beat you to it."

"Hold off." The command came from a different voice. "Who all is with you, nig?"

Choate kept his face to the dirt. To talk wouldn't gain him any escape, but it might give them temper to kill him anyway.

"This don't look like no thief. He wouldn't be alone for just that. By the looks of this rifle, he's out hunting something. Could be us."

"Then let's kill him and be out of here."

"A shot would be heard for miles," the second voice cursed. However, the next words came as calm as talk around a campfire. "No, we're going to keep this one. If there's more out there, they might not be so quick to fire at us. Even if he is a stinking darkie. Tie his hands. If we don't see any more, we'll shoot him in the morning."

The lady sang with great spirit in high tones, occasionally strutting across the stage, arms raised, kicking her legs in one direction, then the other. Cole didn't recognize the song, but the act was one seen before in the dance halls of Kansas and Texas. However, those women weren't as pretty as this gal.

She cast an eye at him for a single second. She didn't smile or interrupt the singing. Never before standing at that place during a show, he took advantage of the view of her back side. The garment couldn't be any tighter than if it were painted on.

She came to the center of the stage, took a wide stance, stretched out her arms, and sang at the top of her lungs the words *"all the way home,"* holding the last note for as long as a minute. She stopped. The music stopped. She bowed her chin to her chest and the curtain next to Cole reeled across the stage. Loud cheers and whistles cascaded through the thick cloth. She raised her head for only a moment to look at him. A grin creased her face. As the curtain parted again, she stood for a second while the men continued to clap, holler, and hoot. In a long, deliberate motion, she curtsied even without a skirt, dipping her head below her knees. The curtain quickly reeled across again, and she scampered over to Cole.

"Hello, Clay," she said, putting on a sheer robe, then shaking one of his bound hands. "I'm Vivien." Her voice held a cut to it as one he had heard from an Englishman in Texas. Before he could ask why he'd been brought there, she took hold of the shackles and led him up a long, steep flight of wooden stairs with lanterns hung on the wall to light the way.

"Miss Hooper," said an older man in a derby and suspenders. "They want an encore."

She didn't look back at him. "Tell them I've retired for the evening."

With his hands in front of him, Cole knew if he didn't keep up with her rapid climb he'd tumble back down the steep stairs. After more than thirty steps, they reached the top. She opened the single door to the only room on the upper floor. Oil lamps hung on opposing walls lit up the room. Partitions of fine fabric stood in front of a table cluttered with a basin, jars filled with different colors, a mirror, and a white iron bathtub with gold painted legs. Another partition was propped in front of a bed the size to sleep double.

"You can wait here. I won't need a moment to get out of my costume," she said, pointing to a chair, then released the shackles to retreat around the partition in front of the tub. Cole sat on the chair, still bewildered as to the reason he was there, although he sensed it was for more than neighborly talk. "There's some sherry on the vanity. Would you pour us some?"

He looked to the table. The request had him reach for a sculpted glass bottle filled with pinkish liquid. The iron chain rattled.

Not wanting to appear an invalid, he rose to stretch his hands as far apart as possible in order to hold the bottle and pull the similarly sculpted top. His fingers strained to remove the top. At first the cork in it wouldn't budge, so he pushed as hard as he could with two fingers. The top edged loose slowly until it popped off from the pressure and bounced on the table in a hail of racket. Embarrassed, he glanced over his shoulder to see if she noticed the noise.

Her silhouette projected onto the fine fabric partition. The figure squeezed out of the corset, shoving the tight garment down one hip then the other repeatedly, until finally it sagged to the thighs and beyond the shadow. The bottom edge of the partition was half a foot above the floor. In full view, the corset crumpled on the rug under her bare feet. He watched as she stood motionless for a single second, admiring all the contours of the female form outlined in shadow against the brighter partition.

His fingers lapsed their grip on the bottle. His jaw slipped ajar. His chest tightened slightly and he felt a shiver run through his spine, sending a ripple over his skin. It had been more than three years since he'd been with a woman, and on only one occasion before had he been the one pursued. He cracked a grin at having thought the notion of being taken from jail meant trouble. If only all his life's troubles came to this end, he'd have sought a reason to be in jail more often.

The figure reached for a robe and wrapped it around her shoulders. "Did you find the sherry?"

His mind came to the present. He looked to the bottle, which he'd let drip on the vanity. "Ah, yeah, I found it," he said in minor panic, desperately searching for a cloth to clean the mess. Finding none such rag, he put the bottle down, pulled his shirttail from his pants, and leaned over the table to dab the spilt liquor. He needed more slack from the shirt, so he unhooked his pants in order to pull it, slipped the bottom two buttons free, and blotted the liquid. Hearing her rustle from behind the partition, he hurriedly stuffed the shirttail under his belt as best as possible with his bound hands. Her voice behind him turned him about.

"I'm ready for a drink." She pulled her long red locks out from beneath the shiny green robe's collar. Her eyes dipped to his bound hands holding the bottle, then to his rumpled shirttail, one side hanging loose where it was unbuttoned above the unhooked pants. "First things first, mate.

Where's my drink?" She came to stand directly in front of him. Taller than most women, she still only stood as high as his nose. Cole snapped the chain shackles, drawing attention to their restriction. "Oh, I see." She drew the key from the robe pocket and murmured. "This could be fun. Very tempting. But I'll take these off only if you promise to behave yourself?"

Cole felt a grin crease his face at the question. "I've always been respectful of what women tell me to do." The smile on her face widened. She slowly inserted the key in the slot and turned. The shackle loosened. She did the same to the other, and he rubbed relief into his irritated wrists.

"My God. What is that?" Her question drew his eyes past his open shirt to the scar above his navel.

"Oh, that's a mark from a knifepoint."

She raised her brow. "A mark? Looks like a bloody gash."

"It was at the time. A fellow had aim on running the whole blade through me, but I kept it from going deeper than it did. A woman doctor stitched it up with a mule's hair. Hardly notice it now." He continued to rub his wrist, when she grabbed his left hand and turned his palm up to see another scar, which ran from the forefinger to the heel.

"Another one?"

He nodded. "Same reason. Different fellow."

She tossed the iron on the table and poured the liquor in two tall-stemmed glasses. "You sound like a dangerous man, Clay." Once both glasses were full, she picked up one and offered him the other. "I like dangerous men." He took a sniff. The liquid smelled like liquor, but it was not as pungent as corn whiskey. His hesitation drew her notice. "A problem? Don't you like it?"

"I swore off whiskey a long time ago."

"Why is that?"

He pondered the question. "It turns me mean. Something I didn't like."

"Well," she forced him to take it, "this isn't whiskey from saloons. It's wine. I think you'll like it. Have a taste."

He took another sniff. It reminded him of some red liquor he enjoyed from that Englishman. That didn't have the burn of corn whiskey then, so he took a sip. The taste wasn't as tart as before and held no real burn as he swallowed. It brought to mind another similarity. "You a foreigner?"

She grinned. "How'd you guess?"

Her sly grin didn't seem genuine, but he answered as if it were. "I met up with an English fellow about a year ago in Texas. He had the same cut to his words as you. Sounds like you're asking a question when you ain't. You from there?"

She wandered over to the tub. "No. I'm from Australia. A little place in Queensland called Doone's Ferry. Later, I moved to Sydney."

He took another sip and scratched his chin. "I don't rightly know where that is."

She huffed a giggle. "It's the other side of the world." She moved the partition away from the tub and stepped around to the far side. "It takes almost two months on a ship to get there." She put down her glass and bent to lift something out of view; however, she straightened empty-handed and looked at him. "Would you help me?"

Shamed on manners, he put down his glass and went to her. On the other side of the tub were two full buckets of water with steam rising from each. She motioned for them to be poured in the tub, and he did so carefully so as to not splash from the bounds of the rim. "Where'd you get hot water?"

"I ordered them to be brought here ten minutes before the end of the show."

He huffed a laugh as he finished pouring the first bucket. "Hot water. You must hold rank to order something that special to be toted all the way up here." He picked up the second bucket.

"You'd be surprised what a little fame can get you 'toted' up here. It got you here."

He dropped the bucket into the tub. The brazen words had him stand in confusion for only a second. She giggled at his clumsiness. He bent and removed the floating bucket. Not in his entire life had he been with such a forceful woman with the beauty of this one that didn't want money for her attraction. Again, he felt a lapse of manners. "I guess you'll be wanting me to leave now so you can take your bath."

"No. The bath is for you."

Again, he stood dumbfounded. "Me?"

She nodded with sincerity. "Yes, you." She pulled the partition between them. "Although I'm not strong on formality, I am a lady. I assume you can undress yourself. But if you need help, just give a whistle." She pulled the fabric wall to block her view of him.

Cole stood bewitched by this woman's charm, beauty, and nature for mischief. In the past, he'd had his share of whoring with the gals in the cattle towns of Kansas, but those encounters were brief and to the business at hand. This one didn't look the type. He glanced at the surroundings. This wasn't a cathouse room. Besides, she hadn't even mentioned money and must have noticed he was in no way to have any. All the wondering only confused him more.

"How far along are you?"

Her patience sounded as slim as her waist. Just as with the notion of a good rest, he resigned himself to the pleasure afforded him and unbuttoned his dark green shirt. With it off, he began unthreading the laces of his tanned hide leggings. "Getting to it," he answered. "Got more than a single corset to deal with."

"Ummm," she cooed. "You're a devil tease."

He continued removing the leggings and then slipped off the boots themselves. Wool socks were next, then the unbuckled belt from the pants. Once loose, he freed the rest of the buttons of his pale brown dungarees. He slid them down past his knees, then yanked them from each leg. A moment's thought was given to leaving his drawers on and slipping into the water. They needed a wash, too. A second thought cleared his mind of the notion. This was no pond water. No sense getting clean and wearing filthy drawers. He threaded the button free and slid the linen from his hips and legs. After a deep breath, he stuck a foot in the steamy water. A momentary cringe from the heat soon passed, as it did with the other foot, so he settled his body, butt first, into the tub and reclined in the soothing relief.

Vivien pushed the partition aside. "It's about time." Her scowl grew to a smirk. She handed him the glass of pink liquor. "Enjoy that." He took the glass while she retrieved a small jar from the table, then came to kneel next to the tub. Once nestled, she peeked into the water at the area below his waist, then raised her eyebrows. "Not bad."

Cole's mind wandered between shyness and pride. "Not bad? Something tells me this ain't the first time you've had a man in this tub."

"You're wrong on that," she answered, opening the jar and spilling powder into the water, brushing the surface as she poured. Soon, foamed bubbles emerged like yeast in bread. "You're the first in this one. But not the first man I've had to clean." She took a washcloth from the table, returned to her knees to soak it in the water and wiped his chest and arms, soaping his skin like a saddle, then rinsed his body by wringing the cloth.

Her admission invited more questions. "Just who are you?"

She showed him a puzzled face. "I thought you knew. My name is Vivien Hooper. Viv for short."

"I heard that much. What you doing here?"

A contented smile came over her face. "Why am I in the hills of America with a strange man in my bathtub. Is that the question?" She took a cake of soap from the floor, dipped it in the water, and rapidly rubbed it between both hands for lather.

"Something like that." She swabbed the lather on his face. He reared his head. "Whoa! What are you doing?"

"Don't be a baby. You look like an animal." She continued swabbing. "I'm a singer. I always wanted to sing. I sang for my parents and then their friends at home." She smeared the soap about the other cheek, then stopped. Slowly, she brushed the scar above his right eye. "What happened there?"

The memory from long ago came to mind. "That's the mark of a slug nearly took my life."

"When?" she asked, tenderly running her fingertips over it.

"Near three years back. Some bank robber on the run from a posse in New Mexico

78

bushwhacked me for my clothes. Once he had them, he thought about ending me while I put on his duds."

Her smirk returned. "So this isn't the first time you've been ordered out of your clothes, Clay?"

He huffed a chuckle. "No. A ten-year-old boy kept me from drowning in a couple inches of water then. His ma took me in, tended to my wound, fed me, gave me a place to sleep." Vivien froze stiff at the mention. "Outside."

Vivien resumed lathering his cheek. "Sounds like a fair dinkum woman. What about her husband? Did he mind you there?"

The somber memory of living with Ann Hayes and her children in Nobility, New Mexico, draped his good mood. "She was a widow." The lathering slowed. "She was being run off her land by the railroad. Had her barn burned down." He dipped his eyes to the water. "I enjoyed helping them." A brighter memory entered his head. "Me and the boy, Noah, we built a new barn together." He felt her hand spread the soap down his throat.

"A barn? So she kept the land?"

He bobbed his head once. "I think so. I was able to get them some money to buy the land outright."

"Think so? What kind of a gentleman are you, Clay? Didn't you stay and see it out?"

"No," he said with some sadness. "I had to go." He looked into her eyes. She held an arched brow, but it soon eased.

"That's too bad." She rose, went to the table, and returned with a folded straight razor. While standing before him, she pulled the robe from her shoulders and let it sink to the floor. He gazed at her figure in the sheer lace shimmy. The shade of her fair flesh bled through the lace garment down to the sparse red tint at the bottom. The sight stole his breath and sent a tingle through his nerves from his chest past his waist and all the way to his toes.

She peeked into the water at his masculine reaction to her pose and arched an eyebrow. "Getting better." Again, she knelt next to the tub and unfolded the razor. "So tell me, Clay. Are you some bandit like a Ned Kelly or something?" She put the edge to his throat.

"Who?" Again he reared his head. "Be mindful with that. You know what you're doing?"

"Be still." She scraped off a swath of whiskers. "When one is in the show business, one must shave more delicate spots."

She dipped the blade in the water and shook the lather free from the blade. "Ned Kelly is a robber back in Australia." He felt another scrape of whiskers gone and heard another shake of the razor in the water. "Rumor has it, he was hung for his crimes. Shot a policeman. A nasty bloke, they say. But others said he was just doing it to feed his poor family."

Cole kept his head stretched back to make an easier target for the razor. "I can give mind to the notion that people say what's easiest to believe, and not the truth." The blade moved to his right cheek. "So did they hang him or not?"

"I don't know. When I left, the newspapers reported he was alive." While she rinsed the razor, he faced her full.

"When was that?"

She turned his face straight. "The spring of eighteen-eighty. September third to be exact." When he jerked his head, she pulled the blade back with a look of disgust.

"Wait. Spring ain't in September."

Once more, she pushed his head straight. "It is in Australia. Below the equator, the seasons are switched from America."

The idea seemed a fool's belief. "How they do that?"

She stopped and rubbed the back of her fingers gently along his now-smooth right cheek. Her voice now carried some sadness. "Because it's a long way away. Trust me."

Cole gave mind to that notion as well. She reached across his face to shave his left cheek. "So how long you been here?"

"I arrived in San Francisco in January of last year."

"San Francisco. I keep hearing folks talk about the place."

She leaned closer. A hint of a smile creased her lips. "Lovely place it is. The whole town is perched on a steep hill over the bay."

"Then why ain't you there now?"

She didn't answer immediately, taking time to clean the razor. Again she reached across his face. "San Francisco is a very big city. A lot of performers there. Instead of competing for the same audience, my agent sent me east to the mining towns where lonely men are starved for the sight of a woman."

He nudged his head, fearing a full nod would get him cut. "A fine-looking woman."

She smirked at the compliment while continuing to draw the razor. "The problem is that there are so few fine-looking men."

The remark humbled him, so he nodded. "I'll take that to mind, too." She giggled, slightly angling the blade's edge, nicking his jaw. Her face changed to a look of regret.

"Look what you made me do." Gently, she took his jaw between her fingers. "No worries, though." Gradually, she lowered her lips to the wound and applied a slow kiss upon it. "I'll make it better." She planted another one, leaving several more down his throat, then met his eyes. "I find you a fine-looking man, Clay." Her kiss to the other side of his chin sent the wind of a bull through his lungs. "A very fine-looking man," she whispered.

"It's been a long time."

"Be quiet," she answered in a breathy tone, then tenderly kissed his lips. She tasted warm, moist, with the flavor of a spicy pepper.

He reached for her waist. She was eager to join him in the tub and climbed astride his lap. The flimsy strap of her shimmy slipped from her left shoulder, drooping enough to reveal that her breast matched her slender frame.

Instinct had him cup it to suckle at the taut nipple. He sensed she didn't mind when she wrapped her arm around his nape and clutched him closer. While he tasted the soft flesh again and again, she freed her other arm from the garment, then grabbed his wet hair and clamped her lips onto his. She took his hands beneath the surface to guide them to her naked hips, where the shimmy had collapsed. She released his lips only long enough for him to peel the wet garment from her body and over her outstretched arms.

She rolled about to lie back against his chest, sending waves lapping out of the tub. Her right palm found his right cheek and she drew it near to nibble at his lips and stab her tongue between them. He brushed her long soaked strands from her face, then filled his palms with her breasts.

His blood was at full boil. By now he'd be done with some town tart, having relieved the throbbing in his loins. Never had he had a woman who wanted a man worse than he a woman. First nature had him attempt entry, but she moved from its path. Instead, she took the back of his right hand into hers. Slowly, she glided their hands along her glistening white belly and below. She led his finger into bristled hair to touch her delicate folds. His fingertip found her mound of flesh. She rolled her head to the side upon his touch, staring him in the eye. Her finger atop his, she increased the pace of his caress. While she continued, her chin fell ajar, her breath at a pant, eyes piercing into his, brow furrowed. Her features showed sheer terror or pure delight. Unsure which, he eased the pressure and pace until she gripped his hand like a claw and edged her mouth near his ear to speak in a breathy stammer.

"More."

He complied with her request, himself driven to frenzy with primal desire. She whimpered and groaned at his stroke.

Her hand sank beneath the surface and found his aroused private by delicately wrapping her fingers around it in a tender tug. His heart pounded through his ribs as they locked eyes. Now he inhaled deeply to stall the end. She arched her back slightly, lifted her hips atop his, and eased lower. She rocked back and forth while their fingers maintained mutual touch at her spot. Her head craned back, her lips brushing his. "Take me to bed, Clay."

Just as with an order to attack, he didn't hesitate. He rose out of the bath, lifting her into his arms. Water dripped on the wooden floor as he carried her to the bed. She sank into the mattress. Her cheek against the sheet, she didn't alter her position and reached behind to grip the back of his thigh so to keep him in preferred place. She wanted him to continue as they started in the tub. His length ran full into her. Her groan resonated through the linen.

His hands slid to her hips. She forced herself against him in firm, rapid strokes. Every nerve sparked like embers, tingling his spine. She quickened her pace, each thrust faster than before, sending a rush through his loins and releasing with throbbing pulses.

They collapsed onto the bed side by side, his chest to her back, just as they had lain in the bath. Vivien let out a long-held breath. "I waited three years for that." She reversed her position to face him and planted a peck on his lips.

Cole, still catching his breath, rolled onto his back and she put her head on his chest. The rush in his blood and nerves slowed into a soothing and relaxed calm. "About the same for me." Moments passed before he felt her hand sweep his chest and belly. A finger found the old wound on his left hip.

"My God! What happened here?"

He couldn't think of a better explanation than the truth. "That's the hole a .44 slug makes on its way out. There's a smaller one on my back where it went in."

"During the American war? As a soldier?"

He exhaled in disgust of the reason and muttered, "Bounty hunter."

"My God, Clay. Bullet wounds, knife scars

86

— it's a bloody wonder you're still alive and have all your pieces about you." He smirked, thinking how often he'd thought the same. She paused before resting her head in the crook of his shoulder. "Why are you called the Rainmaker?"

The often-asked question closed his eyes. "It's a name my ma called me when I was little. When I was trooping, the officers heard about it from my pa. He was a captain, killed in the war." He stopped, recalling the day he watched his pa die in a grassy field in Texas. "Anyway, once the enlisted men found it out, they all kept calling me that. I guess for some it was easier to remember."

"My name is Vivien Earnestine Hoogenpuhl," she admitted softly. "But when you're in the show business, that's too much for people to remember. And too big for the bills plastered on the walls. So my agent told me to take the name Hooper instead. My father never forgave me for that." Her voice held the same regret. "Did I tell you that my parents were from America?"

"Don't recall you saying that."

"They were. My father met my mother aboard a ship bound for the gold fields of Victoria. My grandfather died soon after arrival in America, so my mother told me. She latched on to my father, who left California after the gold played out there. He didn't find any. So he spent the last of his money and went on to Australia. They finally settled north in Queensland." She paused to giggle. "My mother said they were married proper before I was conceived. But I counted the months back from my birth. I figured I came about near the ship's turn 'round Melbourne. Despite the time not being right, my mum insisted she was still a virgin when she married. She didn't like me questioning her about it. Said such thoughts would put the devil in me. I guess she was right. Look at me now. Did your mum figure you'd be here?"

"There was a story she'd tell. About how when I was born, a pawnee squaw saw in my eyes a future. She told my ma that I was a bringer of the rain. A maker of miracles."

Vivien lifted her head back at him wearing a smile. "I'll attest to that." Again she pecked his lips. "I'll vote you a fair dinkum." She rose out of bed and went to the vanity. As he watched her naked figure retrieve the stemmed glasses and refill them, he pondered just what his future had in store.

He'd traveled throughout the West for near seven years, avoiding the law due to a claim of treason that few knew was false.

Still, just as he admitted, the easier story for folks to believe was the loudest one heard.

She handed him the glass and sat on the edge of the bed. As she sipped, he tried to ration the fact that he presently shared the bed of a beautiful red-haired woman. While staring at her and she at him, he swigged the tasty liquor, in part as an act of defiance to his future fate.

She cast a coy eye at him, put down her glass, and took the empty one from his hand to do the same. She crawled in bed and retook her position next to his side. While leaning close to his face, she planted a tender peck while her hand once more swept his chest and then his belly. "Are you ready for an encore?" He was unsure of the word, but her meaning quickly became plain with the next destination of her fingers. However, his mind wasn't attentive, and therefore neither was the rest of him. Her finger's gentle tease slowly changed his mood. "Not bad," she said. "But let me make it better." With that, she settled her breast across his belly.

As the moist warmth once more sent a tingle through his nerves, he closed his eyes and relieved his mind of his fate in the future, enjoying the pleasure of the present.

CHAPTER FIVE

Cole rolled his shoulders to resettle his position. He almost fell from the bunk. The imbalance tore him from his sleep. Blinking in the daylight, he slowly focused upon the interior of the jailhouse office. He closed his eyes again, sure that he was lost in a dream, but when he opened them, the office was still there.

"Hey," he called to Sheriff Stillman, who sat at the desk doodling on papers. "How'd I get here?"

The lawman appeared puzzled. "You gone fool? You came in day before yesterday. With Choate. Don't you remember?"

Cole shook his head, then noticed his shirttail pulled from the pants waist, his boots in the corner of the cell. "No. That ain't what I'm talking about. You took me across the street last night. To the theater. Left me with Vivien Hooper, the red-haired singer."

Stillman turned to face him full. A sly grin grew on his face until it became a wide gleam followed by a low to high guffaw. "You don't say?"

Cole shook his head again, himself puzzled at the lawman's surprise. "Hell yes, I do say. Last night, you took me in shackles to watch her show. You left me there, and we went upstairs to her room, and . . ." Stillman leaned forward in the chair, elbows on his knees and an eyebrow arched. Cole felt he was revealing more than a proper gentleman should about his private evening with the lady. "Well, you left me to watch her show. You got to remember." Stillman shrugged. Cole sat up on the bunk. Instantly, his head pounded as if a blacksmith had hit him flush with a hammer. He recalled the taste of a different liquor, but couldn't recall how much he drank. The amount wouldn't have to have been considerable to have the effect. "Damn. If you don't remember, you old fool, go and ask her."

Stillman, still with his smile in place, looked to the front door. "I guess I would like to hear the rest from her, but she left town early this morning on the Wells Fargo."

The news hurt worse than a kick to the gut. "She what?"

"She left. Stage came through early this morning. She came out all dressed like it was Sunday, climbed into the stage, and it pulled away a few minutes later."

"Where'd she go?"

The sheriff scratched his chin. "I believe I heard she was headed to Butte. I heard the driver nagging while loading the trunk on top about how he didn't think it would stay there the whole trip." Stillman rose in his chair. "I was just going over to the hotel to have lunch. Can I fetch you something?"

Cole was lost in a stare.

"I said, do you want something to eat?" The sheriff's irritated tone brought Cole out of his trance, and he shook his head. "Suit yourself. I shouldn't be long. The cell is unlocked if you need to make trip to the privy." The door opened and shut. Cole leaned against the wall.

What he had heard was hard to swallow. The lawman had acted as if the night's event never happened. At first, he shook the notion from his mind. He was sure it had. The old sheriff appeared fond of playing with people's minds. It could be likely that he was being played with from the start, in the same manner as when he was taken from the cell. Or was he even taken from the cell?

The throb in his head was familiar. It was an old memory, but one he knew well from his days of sucking on a bottle like a mother's tit, often leaving him with the pounding ache between his temples. At first he was not fond of spirits, but it was the only remedy that dulled his mind from the loss of Polly and the baby he put in her belly. Fire swept through their shanty before she had a chance to escape. Nearly six months passed before he was able to push away the smell of liquor, and since then he kept control of the demon for eight years.

Had he mistaken the strong taste in the coffee for whiskey from the morning before? It might explain the throb, but it didn't give him peace of mind as to why the spicy taste of the redhead lingered on his lips. Nor did it take away the softness of her flesh. Those memories were as real as any he'd experienced.

He inhaled deep, closed his eyes, and blew out in a huff. Perhaps his own mind was playing tricks, yet his senses recalled Vivien Hooper's delicate touch, her pleasing scent, and her voice whispering in his ear. However, if he had shared her bed, why didn't he recall the return trip to the cell? Even if the pinkish liquor had gotten the best of him, that creaky-boned sheriff wasn't able to tote him back to the jail bunk. Who put his clothes back on his body? If he walked back on his own, did he forget the trip across the street? The puzzle troubled his mind, and he scratched his chin. It took a moment before he noticed the lack of whiskers.

He rubbed harder, then ran his fingers over his cheeks, also barren of any stubble. Relief and delight exhaled out of his head as well as his lungs. His eyes still closed, he enjoyed the certainty of sanity and the remembrance of his evening with the red-haired lady from some far-off place named Australia.

The rattle of the front door raised his eyelids. The young reporter happily barged into the office with a smile. "Good afternoon," he greeted, removing his derby.

The announced time of day brought the throb back to Cole's head. A childhood on a farm had given him the habit of waking before dawn. Liquor always caused him to sleep late. "Afternoon?"

Richard took a watch from his pocket and flipped open the cover. "Just a minute past twelve." He continued toward the cell and took a seat. "I ran into Sheriff Stillman. He said I could come and finish our little talk from yesterday."

"Little talk?" Cole rubbed his head. "The way my head hurts, I'd like as little talk as I can." He propped a socked foot on the edge of the bunk and wondered who took the time to slip it on.

"Well, actually I just have a few questions." Richard parted pages of a leather-bound book and took a pencil from his pocket. "We were speaking about your time with James Butler Hickok. Wild Bill, as he was called."

"Why do you want to know?"

Richard shrugged. "Because of the reasons I stated yesterday. People in the East are enamored with the legends of the West."

"Legends," Cole scoffed, "that is another name for lies."

Richard blinked a few times while looking to the floor, then looked to Cole. "I was always taught that a legend is a story everyone accepts to be true but cannot prove."

Cole pondered what the young man said. "Well, there is a lot to be said that's true about J. B."

The admission was like a call to dinner for the reporter, who eagerly poised his pencil like a gun aimed at the pages. "Such as?"

The easiest recollections came first to mind. "Well, he was prone to be drunk on more than one occasion. In fact, he was seldom sober, especially when I rode with him. Liked to bed married women when their husbands were away. Was such a poor cardplayer, he often had to run off the winner at the point of a pistol just to keep his money."

Richard shook his head and closed the book. "No, no. I can't write about those stories."

"It's the truth."

"Yes, but people don't want to know those things about a legendary figure. They want to learn how brave he was. Keen of mind, his chivalry, how gentlemanly he was in the presence of ladies."

Cole shook his head. "I thought we were talking about J. B. Hickok."

"Yes, we are. But there must be many other stories that you have to tell. If I was to submit an article conveying the type of behavior you mention, my editor wouldn't print it and probably wouldn't accept another story from me."

Cole inhaled. "That sounds like a whole lot of excuse to make something up. Like lying."

"Not really," Richard said, leaning back in the chair. "There are a few instances we may embellish, but . . ."

96

"There you go saying words that only you understand. All I know is what I remember."

Shoulders slumped, Richard blinked a few more times. "And that's all you remember."

"Might be more." Cole shrugged. "I'll try to put my mind to it." He looked to the window and the rays of sunlight projected on the wall. "Hey, might you have seen me on the street last night? Maybe late at night?"

Richard looked to the front window. "I don't seem to recall." He cast a sly eye at Cole. "However, I might be able to recall if I put my mind to it. Like maybe all the way across the street, or was it someone else? I may not be sure."

Cole exhaled in a huff. "All right. I see what game you're playing. I can say this about J.B. Hickok —"

The front door swung open. Stillman marched through the office and directly to the cell, with a rumpled hat in his hand and without a neighborly smile. "I need to talk to you, Clay. Something awful's happened."

Cole curled an eyebrow in confusion. The hat wasn't his, and it wasn't like he hid it. "How's that?"

Stillman took a deep breath. "Coy Dallas has left his mark."

"What are you talking about?"

"Ben Leonard just rode young Billy Coopman into town. Took him over to Mrs. Courtwright's to be with her boy." He paused and swallowed hard. "Billy ran over to Ben's saying how some men had come to his pa's place. Ben went there this morning. They found Jack Coopman hung from his own tree."

"Oh my God," Richard uttered in awe.

"Sounds like a mean fellow. But why are you telling me?"

"I need your help to go after him."

Cole let loose with a chortle. "Sheriff, you seem to forget that I'm behind bars."

"I can fix that."

"Just the same," Cole said, shaking his head. "I ain't no lawman. That's your trouble, not mine. I have no feud with this fellow Dallas."

The sheriff again took a long breath and nodded. He raised the hat and gave it a quick glimpse before tossing it between the bars. Cole caught it. "Recognize that? You should. It's Choate's."

Cole's chest tightened while he eyed the hat. Every second he remembered an aspect about it, confirming the sheriff's claim.

"Ben Leonard found it not far from the body. He thought it might have belonged to the men who did it. But I saw it was

Choate's." The sheriff turned to Richard. "Let us have the room, sonny."

The reporter took a moment before rising, his face still etched with disbelief. Stillman watched him until he left the office, then pulled a chair to sit in front of the cell.

"When Dallas was found guilty of robbing the Western Flyer of a mine payroll and the murder of three guards, he was sentenced to hang. He made a threat while he was being hauled off to the county jail before they took him to Deer Lodge." Stillman swallowed hard again. "He swore to personally hang every one of the jury. Most didn't think much of it at the time. A lot a prisoners say things they can't get done just out of pure spite. Now the whole county is in a panic."

Cole flung the hat to the side of the bunk. "Why you need me?"

"Most of the men on that jury live all throughout the county. They got to be warned. It wouldn't be Christian to not get word to them that their lives might be at stake. And I'm too damn old to make it in time."

"I ain't no errand boy," Cole said, shaking his head.

"You the only one I got around here that can get there and . . . and . . ."

"And what?"

Stillman stared straight into Cole's eyes. "And kill that son of the devil if you two meet up." He pointed to the hat. "He's got Choate. No telling what he's done with that half-breed, but I know he's got no like for anyone with skin that ain't white. The trouble is, both halves of Choate are the wrong color. We already know what he's done to one white man. But, as far as I know today, there's been no black body found."

Cole turned to the hat. He didn't track down men, not even redskins when he was in the Army. The trade of bounty hunting sickened him. Thoughts of those on his own trail boiled his blood; he knew they'd shoot him in the back for the equal of two years' wages.

He tried to steer his eyes from the hat but could not. It was his friend out there. It wouldn't be a bounty sending him after Dallas. Two days before, he'd offered to go and help. His time under a roof with regular cooked meals had spoiled him. He couldn't let it cost the life of Jenks's son.

At first he glanced at the bars in front of him and motioned his head to the side. "So open the door."

A grin slowly grew across Stillman's face.

He popped out of the chair. Cole slid on his boots. The door was left to swing open while Stillman retreated to the desk. Once the bottom drawer was open, he removed the Colt pistol and gunbelt holster.

"You'll be needing this," he said, handing them to Cole. He arched a thumb toward the door. "I'm going over to the mercantile. See if I can arrange a few donations of cartridges, food, and the like."

Cole nodded and the lawman left the office. Cole spotted his black broad-brimmed hat hanging on the wall. As he went to it, he noticed a shaving mug and brush atop the cold stove. Curious, he peeked inside. Lather was inside, but not moist enough to have been made fresh that morning. Behind the mug sat a folded straight razor. His shoulders slumped and the wind seeped from his lungs. Just when he regained some confidence, doubt refilled his mind. He let out a huff and went to the door.

Sunlight and fresh air greeted him on the boardwalk, followed closely by the nagging voice of the young reporter. "Is it true? Are you going after Coy Dallas?"

Cole arched an eyebrow at him, disappointed that the gossip already had spread in the first five minutes. However, there was no sense in denying it. "Better than sitting in jail. Besides, I'm just going to help warn the folks he's after."

"What folks? Who is he after?"

Now he cringed at admitting more than he should. "That ain't for you to know." He was distracted at the view of the opera house across the street. When he averted his eyes to stop teasing his mind, he spotted Stillman coming out of the mercantile. It gave an excuse for leaving the boardwalk and the reporter, but Richard followed close behind.

"Are you leaving now? I mean, leaving today?"

"No sense staying here to get someplace else."

"This is about the boy brought into town." Richard's realization stopped Cole and turned him about. "You're going to warn the others. The others on the jury."

"Damn you, son. You are a nosy fellow."

"I'm a reporter. It's my nature to ask questions." Cole shook his head and resumed his walk. So did Richard. "Besides, the whole town is talking about it. Everyone heard the news."

"Good. The more people that know, the less far I'll have to ride." Cole crossed the street. Stillman's mood didn't appear as bright as it was back in the office. "Did you get the shells?"

Stillman shook his head. "Not enough. Ole Lester says he's got too much outstanding now, mostly from the mine. Can't carry any more on a note from the county. Normally, I couldn't blame him. They never pay their bills."

"I need at least two weeks' supplies, from what you've told me. Bacon, beans, hardtack. Some coffee. More than ten boxes of shells if I meet up with this Dallas."

The sheriff nodded in agreement, trying to soothe Cole's rising temper. "I know, I know. But that's a bill that could come to more than forty dollars. Ain't no one here got that kind of money. Especially this county."

"I'll pay for it." Richard's calm offer turned Cole's and Stillman's heads about. "If I go with you."

"What'd you say, young fellow?" Stillman politely asked.

"I said I'll pay the amount due if I go on the trip with Mr. Cole."

"Oh, no," Cole said with a wave of his hand. "I ain't heading into trouble while dragging some greenhorn behind me. I can't afford to be turning my head when lead is flying."

"I'm not some 'greenhorn' that has to be

mollycoddled. I assure you I won't be any trouble."

Cole shook his head. "Look, son, this is dangerous territory we're talking about here. You bake like a pan of corn dodgers in the day and freeze as solid as the ice on a pond when we get into the mountains. There won't be no time to be turning back when the conditions don't suit your taste."

"The boy could help you, Clay," Stillman said.

"Help? Help get himself killed?"

"For your information, I made it here riding for one hundred miles from Virginia City. That after having traveled by train all the way from Chicago. I am used to hardship, I can assure you. I won't be any trouble. If you find me to be a nuisance, you can leave me behind. You have my word."

Stillman smiled at the offer. "The boy's got sand, Clay. What'd you say?"

With a long huff, Cole turned his head to the side. His mind flooded with recollections of other easterners he'd taken into unsettled country and how he regretted it every time and swore never to repeat the mistake. However, as he stared at the far mountains, thoughts of Choate crept into his head. If he was to help his friend, he'd have to have the supplies to do it. He faced Richard.

"You get in my way — or worse, force me to take a slug — I promise you I'll breathe long enough to kill you."

Richard smiled. "Understood." He looked to the lawman. "Sheriff, let's get what we'll need."

Cole watched the pair as they happily strode into the store.

CHAPTER SIX

With the sun bending toward the west, Cole peered back at the pack-strapped bay and Richard tightening the cinch on his sorrel. By his gauge, six hours remained in the Montana summer day. Normally, he preferred setting out on trips of this kind at daybreak after a night's rest, but the need to follow Choate's tracks pushed him to the late start.

Confident his gear on the palomino was secure, he gave one last shove to snug the Mouton rifle in the scabbard, then went to inspect Richard's load. At the sight of the long, wooden-legged camera roped to the side of the bay, he closed his eyes and shook his head.

"What'd you expect to do with that?"

Richard glanced at the camera. "Oh, that. I plan to take photographs of the landscape, since we plan to travel into unsettled land. It should be great scenery, don't you think?"

With a stern glare, Cole stared into the young man's eyes and spoke in as calm a tone as he could muster. "We're going after killers and thieves, and all you're thinking about is taking pictures of trees on hills?"

The assessment turned Richard's eyes once more to the camera. Like a child caught in a lie, he stammered for an excuse for the wooden box with a bubbled lens. Further embarrassment was squelched with Stillman's squeaky voice. The lawman handed over a rolled paper.

"Here's a list of the jury. I drew a map of how to get to the Ned Palmer place. It's the closest. Now just one last item to take care of, Clay."

Cole took his eyes off the map and faced the sheriff, who held a six-pointed tin star with the words *U.S. Marshal* etched in the center. "Found it in a drawer from the last one that lighted out of here to go pan for gold in Idaho. I figured them folks on the map may not trust you, but they'll trust this." The lawman pinned the badge to the left side of Cole's chest. The weight of the metal sagged the shirt's cloth. It also pulled at Cole's conscience. For over six years he'd dodged anyone wearing a star. Now he was parading one himself. Stillman continued.

"It will help you out with the Pinkertons."

"Pinkertons?"

"Yeah," the sheriff apologetically acknowledged with a nod. "I heard tell they've been on Dallas's trail since he broke loose. The railroad hired them figuring that Dallas had a vendetta out for them, too."

"I don't like them folks."

"Me neither. But there ain't a thing I can do to stop them. Wearing that badge, they'll have to follow your lead whenever you meet up with them." Cole shrugged and turned for the palomino, when Stillman stopped him once more.

"I need to administer the oath. I'll fill out a certificate later."

"Oath? The last one I swore to was for the troopers. When I found it to be an excuse for killing squaws with kids, I took it back."

"Just the same, you need to swear to this one." Stillman cast a quick eye to Richard. "He can stand witness." The sheriff held up his rigid right palm. Cole let out another breath. He didn't cotton to taking oaths. They were meant to be promises, and he wasn't one to make them. However, it was clear Stillman wasn't about to drop his hand, so Cole raised his.

"Do you solemnly swear to support the Constitution of the United States and the laws of the Montana Territory, and will of true faith bear allegiance to the same and defend the same against all enemies and faithfully and impartially discharge the duties of United States Marshal to the best of your ability, so help you God?"

Cole eyed Richard, then Stillman, and let out a long-held huff. "I guess so. I got no choice."

Confident their presence was hidden by dusk, Coy Dallas stood above the high valley wall, gazing down at his next prey. "There he is," he said, watching the bearded farmer walk through his crop. "Son of a bitch don't even know I'm looking for him."

"How you know that?" asked Tanner, who knelt next to him.

"Look at how calm he is. No shotgun. Looking at his grain. He's worried about coons, not me. The door to his house don't even look bolted. Walking back to his family, the next thing on his mind is supper."

They watched the farmer gradually make his way into his home.

"Coy, I know you want to get back at the people that wanted you dead. But it don't pay no money. What little these folks have hardly is enough to feed the men." Even in the dim light, the hard, cold stare of the short, stocky man could be felt through to the bone. "Don't get me wrong. I want to see these people pay just the same as you." Tanner hesitated, but the men's grumbling needed to be addressed. "It's just that they didn't throw in with you just to hunt down the men on the jury. They want to know when we're going after the mine payroll in Butte."

Dallas turned his face back to the farmhouse. Yellow light could be seen through the cloth curtains. "You tell them, they'll get paid. I know what I'm doing. If it's money they want, they'll have more than they can carry soon. First, I get what's coming to me."

Today I set out on a great adventure. I have been enlisted by the Sheriff of Cantrell County to track down a killer by the name of Coy Dallas. With me as a guide is the former cavalry scout by the name of Clay Cole, who himself is a wanted man for the alleged crime of treason against the army during the Indian Wars. Little ground could be made, largely due to the uneven terrain, which hampered any attempt at a steady pace. Mr. Cole also seemed to be slowed climbing and descending the numerous bluffs, which never seem to end.

"What you writing?"

Richard looked up from his notes. Illuminated in the darkness, Cole knelt next to the fire over the skillet filled with bacon bubbling in grease. Richard laid his pencil between the crease and snapped the book shut. "Oh, I was just making passages in a log I'm keeping." The admission didn't capture the westerner's attention; his focus returned to stabbing the bacon. Since his train of thought was likely lost for the remainder of the night, Richard sat more comfortably on the dust, thinking conversation might pass the time while the bacon sizzled. "So how far do you think we've yet to go?"

Cole scoffed but kept his eyes on the skillet. "We didn't make five miles. At that rate, we'll get to where this Palmer's place is at right about when the first snows hit." He looked up to stare at Richard. "When you're out to get to a place, you travel light. You can't get off the horse to refit your gear every hundred feet."

The reference was understood. The uneven load of the camera allowed the legs to interfere with the sorrel's gait. Richard dipped his head. "I'm sorry for that. Perhaps you can help with the loading of my equipment in the morning?"

Cole stabbed a piece of bacon and stuffed it between the halves of a stale roll. "Better to leave it behind."

"No. You see, it's a very expensive camera. Over two hundred dollars. I just couldn't leave it behind. Besides, I wish to document the trip with photographs, as I said."

"Of trees?" Cole said as he bit the roll in two.

"Not just of trees. I also want to take pictures of the homes we pass. Of the people. Of the lifestyle of the West." Realizing Cole meant to keep chewing, Richard thought it must be every man for himself and took the fork to stab his own piece of bacon.

"Why you so curious about that? Don't people in New York City know how to build a house?"

"Of course," Richard said, shaking his hands from the scald of the hot grease and sliding the bacon slab between the roll halves. "Many of them live in large buildings. Several floors layered atop one another."

"You mean like a hotel?" Cole mumbled while chewing.

Richard nodded once, keeping his eyes on the grease soaking the bread. "You could say that. But much larger than the hotel in Copper Springs. Most of the buildings in New York City are over ten stories." He sank his teeth into the roll and tore off a third. The hot meat had him push the food to each side of his mouth.

"Must be a sizable hotel."

While the bacon sizzled inside his mouth, Richard forced it down his throat, where it left a scorching trail en route to his stomach. He coughed, then, once he had recovered steady breath, Richard wiped the tears from his eyes. "Those aren't hotels, actually. Most of them are tenement buildings. People live in them. Every day."

Cole split another roll and stuffed a crackling slab into it. "How many folks you figure live in that one building?"

Richard looked to the remaining two-thirds of his roll, contemplating whether the pain was worth it. "Hundreds."

"More than a hundred folks living under the same roof?" Cole shook his head, took a healthy bite, and continued to talk with his mouth open. The sight convinced Richard to endure the minor pangs of hunger. "Not for me. I don't think I could stand living with that many folks. It was bad enough in a barracks, with twenty all in the same room. The stink of unwashed feet and snoring at night. Made it hard for a man to get any sleep."

The description planted an unpleasant image in Richard's mind. The swallowed bacon began retracing its path. "Please. No more. I'm beginning to feel ill." He tossed the roll into the dark.

"The food talking back to you?" Cole asked with a grin.

Richard nodded. "That and the mention of twenty pairs of unwashed feet." He took heavy breaths, hoping to remedy his churning stomach. In order to rid the image from his mind, he thought it best to change the subject. "No doubt your love of the open spaces defines your character." When Cole arched a brow signaling confusion, Richard explained. "Your choice to live in this wild country. Sleeping under the stars as we are."

Cole shook his head. "Not by choice. No, you can give me a roof over my head. And a soft bed with a wool blanket in the winter. Ain't nothing to love when you're getting rained on. Not knowing if you're about to be trampled by buffalo."

"Buffalo? I thought they had been exterminated. As a scourge to the railroad."

With a final bite, Cole finished his second

roll. "If you're meaning killed them, then yeah. Killed a few myself. More than ten a day. Some men doubled that with repeating rifles." His face soured as he looked to the fire. "That's another time I ain't anxious to do over. Slaughtering them animals weren't hunting. Most of the carcasses were left to rot in the sun. The Army wanted them killed to starve the northern tribes." He let out a long breath. "And they did. They starved." He again faced Richard. "But there's still enough of them animals around to crush your bones into the mud."

Not wanting to trouble Cole further with pained memories, Richard thought to turn the conversation. "I read that Wild Bill Hickok also worked for the railroad killing buffalo."

Cole stabbed the last piece of bacon. "He did," he said simply.

In hopes of more of an answer, Richard prodded with another question. "Is that how you met him?"

"Not long before that."

The short answer pushed Richard's curiosity. "When was that?" He had to wait while Cole finished the last roll, then wiped his fingers on the back of his trousers.

"Met up with him after I was done trooping. I guess that would have been sixty-eight. A man named Jenks, colored scout, Choate's pa, took me out and taught me scouting. Well, Jenks knew Hickok and we met up with him in Nebraska, killing buffalo."

Richard picked up his book and jotted the facts on the front page. "That's good to know. What else can you tell me?"

"Why you writing this book?"

The question surprised Richard, and he changed his view from the white pages to the reddened face of the frontiersman. "There's a man in New York City who uses the pen name Ned Buntline. Have you heard of him?" Cole shook his head. "Well, a great many people have. He's published the accounts of Wild Bill Hickok and Buffalo Bill. Almost everyone in the East has read these books. It's my hope to attain the same acclaim. Only, Buntline's books have a . . . let's say poetry about them that doesn't reflect the actual truth. I hope to set the record straight."

"And how you going to do that?"

Richard closed the book. "By interviews with the people who know these men. Like yourself."

Cole's brow furrowed. "Listen and hear, son. If your plan was to follow me through this country asking me questions, turning my head around instead of keeping it aimed in front me, you best give it up now. I ain't got no time nor patience to be recalling everything about people I ain't seen in more than ten years. Hell, if you want to know about Hickok, go ask Cody."

The suggestion wasn't one Richard hadn't thought of before. He hung his head and stared blankly at the fire. "I've tried. But he refused to tell me anything. He claimed he had a contract with Buntline. A sort of exclusive arrangement. He was polite about it, but he told me that he was forbidden to be quoted about his adventures to anyone other than his publisher."

As Cole watched the flames, sparks spattered and flew from the crash of new wood he tossed. "Then it sounds like you're out of luck, friend. You might think about turning back for town now before we get too far along."

The suggestion came in a tone of encouragement, like salt in a wound. Richard cringed. Another failure, only this one came after such a long trip from home.

"Well, I have an early start tomorrow." Cole unfurled a bedroll.

The mention had Richard remove his watch from his vest pocket. The hands read a quarter past nine, but the image of Emily was what kept him from shutting the cover. It was the photograph he'd taken shortly after she accepted his proposal. There was no greater time in his life. She allowed her auburn hair to flow on her shoulders for the pose, but only after an hour's pleading. Her youthful face wasn't captured in the image, yet it remained forever pressed in his memory.

"That your woman?"

Cole's inquiry brought him from the past to the present. He nodded. "Yes. My wife Emily."

"Then you're a lucky man. Seems a shame to leave behind a handsome gal like that while you're out here in the Montana brush. If I had that waiting on me, I'd be back in your New York City, closer to her than you are to me." He lay on the bedroll.

The remark brought both a tickle and a sting. "She's not in New York City. She's at home in Chicago."

"Chicago City?"

"Yes. Although I haven't heard it called that before. But, yes, that is where I'm from."

Obviously intrigued, Cole angled himself on an elbow. "Then how come all this talk about New York City?"

The question amused Richard. "When

you have an ambition to be a writer or have your photographs published, there is only one place in the country to strive for. And that is New York City. The largest city in the country — and on the continent, for that matter. It is where most of the culture of the country comes from."

"Then why ain't you living there?"

"It takes a great deal of money to live there." He attempted to repress the deeper reason, but the more he spoke, the less heavy the weight in his chest. He reclined on his own bedroll. "My original vocation was in the medical field. It was what I was trained for in college. Emily also attended." Her early interest in him came to mind but left quickly. "But my heart wasn't in it. The pursuit of medicine is a very rigid field. Those at the top like to keep those of a lower status down. I didn't see much of a future for me in it. There isn't much money in mending broken bones and the study of viruses."

"Sounds like the Army. If you ain't born an officer, the best you can make is corporal." Cole resumed his prone position. "That done it for me. I listened to all the orders I could stand."

"It was the same way for me. However . . ." the confession stuck in his throat, but he forced it out. "Emily felt differently. She's very much a conservative in a man's pursuit of career." He found himself muttering his thoughts. "She sees this as a fool's ambition."

"You mean, you out here with me?"

"Yes," he reluctantly agreed.

"She must see something in it. She let you take off with the family money you're making on it. She don't take notice of you writing for a newspaper in New York City?"

Richard took in a long, hard breath. "The money spent of these supplies was all the money I had. I thought it worth the risk to come along with you. Truth be told, I don't really write for *Harper's Weekly*. I hope to have an established line of submissions. But as of yet, I'm still submitting articles. I've earned nothing from this."

Cole's jaw dropped. "In that case, maybe she's right and you are a damn fool."

Richard felt obliged to defend the action. "The editor there said he would look at something new and fresh. So I'm here looking for just that. Together with actual photographs rather than sketched likenesses of the participants. It is my belief that photography will one day be the way news is brought to the masses. Pictures tell so much more than words, don't you think?"

"Oh, I ain't one to say. Reading ain't never been something I got the hang of."

Richard sat up. "You can't read?"

Cole only glanced at him, then returned his view to the stars. "Nope. There's some words I seen before. Like my name wrote out on paper. But when they're all squeezed together in a long line, I ain't got the patience for it." Again he glanced at Richard. "I leave that to folks like you."

"I could teach you."

"Ain't interested."

"But why? Don't you want to know more about the world around you?"

"Nope. Figure I've gone this long without it, can't make much difference now." He put his hat over his face.

Choate struggled against the rope binding his hands behind his back. The fire lit up the camp, showing the two gunhands across from him. He reclined back against the large boulder to hide his attempt to free himself.

"Morton, why is it we're keeping this nigger?" said one gunhand to the other.

A sly grin preceded the answer. " 'Cause Dallas wants it that way. Going to make this one his personal darkie, I guess." They both chuckled.

"If you ask me, I say shoot him. We ain't

got enough food as it is," said the first one as a tease, then came the false look of surprise. "Oh, I forgot. We ain't feeding this one. He's going to have to catch the lizards crawling on the ground. Better hope he don't catch a snake. Be a shame if he got bit by a rattler. Be no one to suck out the poison." They both hooted louder.

Choate held his tongue. The words of hate were not new. Although he feared neither man or any of their color, more hate words back at them would only fuel their hatred, likely leading to another beating. It was better to continue the cold stare and keep his words in his head.

The approach of horses and later loud cries steered attention to beyond the camp. From out of the dark, the leader of the gang emerged. Close behind, the tall one with blond hair came into view, lugging a blond girl on his hip. The female looked to be about fifteen years of age. She fought against the tall man's grip, but just like Choate, wasn't able to break free. Finally, once they were in the camp with all the gang now surrounding, he dropped the girl almost in the center of the flames. Like a frightened cat, she twisted her view all about, shying away when she discovered Choate at her back.

"Don't fret him, honey," said the tall one with a laugh. "We ain't going to feed you to him." He opened his duster and unbuckled his belt. The giddy mood and tone slid away into a serious growl. "Hold her down, boys."

The girl screamed and rose to run to the edge of the light, until the one called Morton grabbed her, slapping his hand over her mouth. She fought his grip, shaking her head like a hooked fish. The wriggling enabled her to free her mouth enough to bite his fingers. Now Morton screamed, then slapped her to the ground.

Tanner laughed. "She's got spirit, boys."

The girl scrambled to her feet once more. Two more men came from the shadows. They all tackled her to the ground and held her as drovers do to brand cattle. Choate strained against the rope. The sight of five men holding down a limb apiece stoked at his gut. Normally, he didn't care about the fate of white folks. But this was a young life bullied by grown men.

"Make it quick," ordered the leader. "I got business needs settling." He looked briefly to Choate, his face showing no more or less concern than he showed for the girl, then walked farther into the darkness at the other end of the camp.

The tall man stood over the girl, then

dropped to his knees. He reached for her chest. The girl wailed as she jerked against the firm grip of the men. The tall one slapped her. The wail stopped. He clutched the top of her dress and ripped it apart, and did the same with the white cloth at her front. The tall one hooted as he palmed each teat.

"Now it's time to dip into some of that honey." He ripped the skirt from her legs and pulled down his pants. When he lunged at her, Choate faced away. The girl's cries and the men's shouts filled his ears. The only thing he could do for her was use the distraction to free himself. He leaned forward and felt about the boulder for a sharp edge. His fingers crawled about until he found what he sought. He cast an eye as the tall one thrashed away atop the girl, then as all the rest watched, Choate arched his back and rubbed the rope between his hands against the rock.

Slowly, the girl's cries were muffled and the man's groans climbed. Choate rubbed faster, the sounds fueling his pace, his own flesh scratched from the rough surface. At once he felt a small slack, but he wasn't free. In his mind, he imagined the rope worn through to a few strands. He cut through the last strands to the sound of a snap, then spread his arms apart for the first time in a day.

There was no time to soothe his wounded wrists. He looked to the camp for a weapon. He saw the tall one lean back upright, still on his knees, to the cheers of the rest. At the far left, a rifle sat alone. Carefully, he crawled quickly to it, but before it was in his hands, the click of gunmetal crackled into the air.

"Stop or I'll blow your head off!"

All eyes turned to the far side of the camp. The leader ran into the light holding a pistol at Choate's head, slowly guiding the muzzle down to touch scalp as he came to stand above. "What the hell is going on out here?"

"Kill him," yelled one. "Kill him dead, Coy."

"Kill him? Hell, I ought to kill all of you. He got free because none of you were watching him," Dallas yelled back. "Tanner, get off that girl. I told you she would lead to trouble." Choate cautiously turned his head to see the tall one stand and pull up his pants. The others, still with their attention focused on Dallas, eased their grip of the girl. Arms free, she moved her hands to cover her top and bottom.

"This mean we ain't going to get our turn at her, Coy?" asked the one called Morton.

The girl jumped up with the question, grabbing Morton's gun from his holster as she rose. The others drew the revolvers at her but did not shoot. She wagged the weapon back and forth at them, slowly stepping back, careful not to step on her shredded dress, which drooped from her shoulders and dangled near her feet. Her eyes bulged, tears streaming down both cheeks. Blood trickled from the corner of her mouth. Fluid dripped from her nose, which was as red as her face.

"Easy girl," said the tall one with a kind manner. "You're just going to get in more trouble with that. Give that to me and I promise, these men won't hurt you. No one else will jump you."

The girl peered up at him. Her mouth opened to show gritted teeth. With heaving breaths, she raised the pistol at an aim at the tall one. With both thumbs she cocked the hammer, then let out a loud wail like a warrior's chant.

A blast rang out over Choate's head. He flinched from the percussion, but he saw a red bullet hole in the girl's bare chest and then her blank stare before she collapsed onto the dust.

"Damn," Dallas shouted, smoke wisping from the pistol in his hand. "Look at her now. Look what you done!" He lowered the muzzle at Choate and spoke in a low voice. "Look at what you done, nig. Now a young girl is dead. Because of you." He shook his head, but the pistol didn't wander. "I swear, if something wasn't telling me that you were going to do me good later on, I'd send you to join that girl." He looked to the men of the gang. "Teach him a lesson for the girl, but don't kill him. If you do, I'll kill the one that done it. Then tie him back up."

CHAPTER SEVEN

The sun crept over the horizon. Cole stoked the small coals under the coffeepot. The day needed to be started early, but the snoring reporter appeared to need another five minutes. If it was the price for not having the greenhorn nap while in the saddle, allowing for swifter travel, he was a buyer. Once someone was sawing logs it meant they were getting the most rest, or so his ma told.

The lessons learned when he was young had stuck with him to this very day. His mind turned to his years on a Kansas farm. He was not aware of it at the time, but they were the best of his life. At that age, all he wanted was the chance to leave. Stories of far-off places always filled his head with adventure, luring him beyond the fence around the house. However, he never had the courage to go farther than his ma's shout for supper.

While grinning at the memory, he poured himself a tinful and slurped the boiling java, inhaling the mild dawn's breeze and looking out to the haze settling over the field. Soon, the fondness of the years of his youth faded. He was near a thousand miles from that Kansas farm, and more than that in years. The border wars he had fought turned into one between states. The adventure he craved began sooner than he wanted when his ma passed from consumption. When he caught up with his pa, he found himself surrounded by colored soldiers wearing the blue in Missouri.

Smacking lips broke him from the daydream. Richard rustled onto his side. The time had come, so Cole kicked the young reporter's rump. "Sleep is over. Wipe it out of your eyes. Swallow some of this coffee. We need to make some tracks today."

Richard scrambled to set his mind straight. Sitting upright, he rubbed his palms over his cheeks. "My God, you nearly stopped my heart. I thought we were being attacked. Is that how you always wake people traveling with you?"

Cole nodded. "Pretty much so." He slurped more coffee, then wheezed air to cool his scalded mouth. "Better than a bugle in your ears. That's how I was taught the day started."

The droopy-eyed reporter squinted at Cole. "Where are we?" He sniffed the air, then shook his head.

"The same place we was last night."

"What is that repulsive odor?"

It took a moment before Cole recognized what was the source. "Dung," he said, pointing at the fire. "Looked to be from buffalo. Could be from stray cattle, but I doubt it."

Richard rose to his feet like he'd seen a snake. "You use that in a fire?"

Cole refilled the tin. "Better than wood. Catches fire quicker. Burns longer. And a heap more of it." He swept his finger in a full circle. "You see any trees?"

"You didn't use that last night. I would have smelled it." He cringed his nose. "It reeks."

"That's why the fire went out so quick, too. Quit being an old woman and drink some coffee."

The invitation slowly won over Richard, although he stepped around to find the upwind approach. He touched the pot with bare flesh, but snapped his singed fingers back and shook them in the breeze and blew on them. Cole offered his thick gloves. Richard slipped them on and poured the coffee into his cup.

"So how far to this next person's home?"

"On the map it looks to be more than ten miles. I'm hoping it's wrong. It will take most of the day if it's true." He took another slurp.

"When you get there, what are you going to do?" Richard took a slurp, then rapidly blew.

Cole snickered at Richard's pained reaction, then at the question. "I guess I'm going to try tell these folks what they got to do. Even with this badge, it won't be easy."

Once he recovered normal breath, Richard gave him a puzzled face. "And why is that?"

" 'Cause folks ain't going to want to leave their home. Their property. Most that lived out here have done been through renegade bands riding through the territory. When I was with the troopers, we chased a many of them. But there was still folks living on their land. Through the winter, with snow as high as the roof. Through fires burning everything in its way. Drought, anthrax, hail pelting their crops . . ." He paused to shake his head. "I think it might take more than a single marshal to convince them to abandon all they have and leave for town." He tossed what was left in the tin cup into the smoldering coals. Steam sizzled into the breeze.

He snatched his saddle from the ground, slung it over his shoulder, and went to the palomino.

Richard followed close behind. "What if they don't leave?"

Cole threw the blanket on the horse with one hand and placed the saddle across the horse's back. "Then likely is they'll get hurt." He faced about to the young man. "They'll get themselves killed. If someone's wanting them dead, ain't nothing a farmer or lone rancher can do off on their own." He stepped aside to retrieve the rest of his gear. Richard was on his heels.

"Well, can't you explain that to them? Make them understand their very lives are at risk?"

After he emptied the coffeepot, Cole flipped the grill off the fire pit with the toe of his boot and dragged dirt with his heel to snuff the flames. "If the weather don't stop me."

"Weather?"

He pointed to the clear sky at the north. "When it gets still like this at this time of year, most likely it's fixing to get cool. Clouds might build up soon. Winds pick up." He stood in place in front of Richard, who again appeared puzzled.

"Then what are you waiting on?"

Cole stared him square in the eye. "You."

Cole squinted into the distance. The overcast sky, while keeping away the glare, didn't provide much light. Without shadows, it was hard to determine if the terrain ahead was one large mound or a continuation of numerous rolling hills. As he kept the palomino at a walk, he was sure the one constant was the never-ending questions coming from Richard.

"What time of day would you say it is?"

Cole glanced over his shoulder with an arched brow. "You're the one with the watch."

"Yes. But sometimes I find it to run a bit fast. Right now, it says it to be nine-thirty-two in the morning. Do you think that's right, or should I adjust it?"

Cole peeked at the clouds. "Without no sun, I can't tell you for sure." The foolishness of the question needed an equal response. "Might be nine-twenty-eight."

"You really think so?" Richard asked in earnest.

"It's as good a time as any." The frustration in his voice was noticeable.

"I think it important we stay on a steady course." The clop of hooves meant Richard had brought the sorrel up to the palomino's left flank. Cole's eyes remained to the front. "I didn't mean to be a bother. I was just asking because I had read where most frontiersmen were able to gauge the time of day."

"Well, that goes to show you not to trust reading."

Richard paused, then huffed a laugh. "Do you think Wild Bill would have known the time?"

The inquiry irritated Cole. "He carried a watch just like you."

"Yes, I heard he killed a man over it."

"That he did. But it had more to do with a woman than with the watch."

"Why is that?"

"Dave Tutt was the man's name. Tutt won the watch in a game of cards. Hickok took pride in the watch and didn't care for Tutt wearing it hanging from the vest and strutting it like a rooster with a bigger comb, if you know what I mean. Truth behind it all was that Tutt had took to a gal in town that Hickok had been coupling with the year before. The day came around when the two saw each other on the street. The name-calling commenced. Hickok swore to the story that Tutt drew first and fired. The slug hit the ground, then Hickok drew, aimed, and fired." He paused. "Hit Tutt in the heart. Killed him dead that instant. Hell of a shot, so I heard from people claiming to be there. But you know how the more folks telling the story, the better the play gets."

"I had read a similar story," Richard said, then he, too, paused several seconds before asking a question. "Would you have been able to make such a shot?"

Again the query soured his mood. "I never took to bragging when I shot a man. And I never took time to admire the quality of it. I was more concerned with not being a target for those I was shooting at. If I hit them, then it had to be. If I didn't, and they or I turned tail, so much the better."

As they approached the rise, a valley emerged between two slopes. A single shack was visible on the grassy floor. By first appearance, it seemed a small farm. No one was out tending to the fields of wheat. Richard's questions continued as Cole reined back.

"So, as a marksman, would you say that Wild Bill Hickok was a better shot than you? Or others you've known?"

Cole muttered, "He was better than all of us."

Richard came alongside the palomino and stopped the sorrel. "Have we arrived at the Palmer place?"

"Reckon so." He glanced at Richard and nudged the palomino down the slope. During the descent, Cole expected the owner to show himself, a normal act for the approach of strangers. However, when they reached the wheat, only small birds and varmints on the ground scattered between the stalks. He put his right palm on the butt of the Colt revolver.

"What's wrong?" Richard asked.

Cole glared over his shoulder. "Hush your mouth." With a cautious eye toward the surrounding brush, he steered the palomino to the house. No smoke came from the stovepipe. Slowly, he dismounted, still with a grip on the pistol butt.

"Hello in the house."

There was no reply. The windows showed a dark interior. No glow from lit lanterns could be seen, which was peculiar for such a gloomy sky. Again he called out, and again his answer was silence.

He took a deep breath, convinced the only answers lay inside. He turned about to the young reporter. "You stay here." He drew the Colt. "If you hear gunfire, ride the other way." Richard's eyes widened, but there was no time to calm the kid's nerves. Angling his shoulders, Cole stepped up on the porch. He took another deep breath before he turned the latch and pushed open the door.

In a rush, he stepped inside, the Colt at arm's length, sweeping from one corner to the next. No one was inside.

Two of four chairs lay on the side. No dishes were on the table. A blanket hung spilt from the bunk in the loft above. Cole lit a lantern and walked the interior for any sign of what had happened. Whatever had occurred, it seemed sudden. Clothes were still hung on hooks. Drawers to the bureau remained shut. As he made his way out of the shack, a color on the floor stopped him.

Cole knelt next to it and shined the lantern near. The tattered blue cloth had frilled white lace at the end, like a cuff. Convinced it was a woman's sleeve, he picked it up and stuffed it in his pocket. Seeing no other sign of a fight, he walked out the door.

The instant needed for his vision to adjust to the brighter outdoors put him at a disadvantage as he focused on six armed men, all aiming rifles and pistols at him. His right hand froze, knowing a further move would send lead his way.

"There he is," shouted Richard from the ground, arms pinned behind his back by the weight of a heavier man's knee. "Tell them, Clay. We're not robbers."

"Throw down your weapon," came an order from the shortest man, wearing a bowler, brown coat, and scrubby whiskers more than two weeks old. He held no gun, but appeared in command of the rest.

Slowly, Cole edged back his coat, revealing the holstered Colt. With delicate finger touch, he drew the revolver.

"He's a marshal," said one of those steadying a rifle. With the announcement, the man raised the barrel's aim to the sky. Confused by the action, Cole peeked down at the tin star pinned to his shirt. Not accustomed to it or the rank it provided, he did his best to react in the proper manner.

"I told you," Richard angrily shouted. "We're looking for the people who own the property."

"Let him up," Cole ordered in a loud tone. As with a private to an officer, the large man kneeling on the young reporter looked to the shorter man in front. A single nod was all that was needed to have the man stand and free Richard. The man in front approached, now with a friendlier face.

"I apologize, Marshal. We came up and saw two horses and only one man." He extended his hand. "My name is Donald Keesler. I'm with the Pinkerton Detective

Agency."

A chill went through Cole's spine with the introduction. Pinkertons were known to dispense justice according to the needs of who was paying. They were the law of the East, the railroads, and banks that didn't like common folk interfering with making money. There was no telling what they knew about all and any men with reputations.

Richard walked to the porch, rubbing his sore wrists. "I think more than a simple apology is needed. They almost killed me, throwing me off the horse to the ground."

Keesler turned his head to the reporter and spoke in a dismissive tone. "And you are?"

"Richard Johnson. I'm a reporter with *Harper's Weekly.*" He pointed a finger at Cole. "And this is —"

"Hayes," Cole blurted, casting a stern eye at Richard to be silent. "Marshal Clay Hayes."

"Pleasure to know you, Marshal. As I said, we didn't mean to harm anyone," he said with a sneer aimed at Richard. "We're on assignment to catch a killer and his gang. Coy Dallas."

"We're here to do the same."

Cole's answer was met with a raised brow

of surprise. "You two? Just you two?"

"That's right. We came out of Copper Springs. A boy told a story that his pa was hung by bandits. It sounded like this fellow Dallas, so we're out here to catch him."

"I learned of the same story. Pity more couldn't be done to save that man or these two here. But I am surprised that there are only two of you. Especially only one lawman and, uh, a writer."

"I'm here to document the exploits of the search," Richard sniped. "And to assist any way I can."

The bold proclamation was met with a contemptuous grin and a shake of the head from Keesler. "Assist?"

The contest of words needed to be stopped before too much was said. Cole wanted little to do with hired gunmen acting as the law. It was one of those words Keesler said that could change the subject. "You mentioned 'these two.' Do you know what happened here?"

The detective nodded and pointed to the end of the wheat field. "Out there, about a quarter mile, are the bodies of a man and a woman. They appeared to be the owners." Keesler huffed a breath. "They look to have been strangled. My guess is they were drug by horses with ropes around their throats."

Richard winced with the news.

The discovery inside stirred Cole's curiosity. "Where you say they are?"

Again Keesler pointed. "At the end of the field."

"Well, then let's go there," Cole said, walking to the palomino. The rest of the Pinkerton group mounted, as did Richard, and all rode the short distance to the end of the field. When the first riders pulled up, Cole slowed the palomino and slid off the saddle. Quickly, he realized he was the only one afoot. He took this as part respect for the badge he wore and part the miserable duty of the law to examine the scene.

The dusty brown coat of the man was easy to see amid the green surrounding grass. Cole knelt next to the corpse and swatted away the horseflies lighting on the face. Palmer appeared a man the same age as himself. He had a full head of hair and burly beard, bloodshot eyes; the skin had turned blue around the neck, leaving a lighter shade on the face and puffed-out cheeks. Just as the Pinkerton man had said, it seemed the neck didn't break at first, causing the rope to slowly crush the throat.

A small distance away lay the woman. Cole walked toward the body, confused at her yellow dress. She, too, showed signs of having had a rope around the neck. Only when he moved her head did he sense the limpness from the body; only the skin and stretched muscle kept her from being in two pieces. By all appearance, her neck had snapped with the first jolt. If there was any good to be seen, it was that she died quickly.

"One's thing for sure. Who done it weren't after butter and egg money. Who would do such a thing?" he muttered as he stood.

"Who, you ask?" replied Keesler from his horse. "Coy Dallas, that's who. The man is a crazed killer, and he must be hunted down and killed or he'll spread out all over this territory and keep killing. Like a wild animal."

There was little to argue over until Keesler continued.

"Marshal, I think we need to get back on Dallas's trail as quickly as possible, before he has a chance to hide in the hills to the west."

Cole shook his head. "I ain't leaving these folks to be gnawed on by vermin."

"Your sense of morals is admirable, Marshal Hayes. But it will take the rest of the day to bury the bodies. These people will have died in vain if we don't find their killers. Once we have Dallas in jail, there'll be time to inter the remains properly."

"I said, I ain't leaving them." Cole peeked at the sun. "Besides, I think them that done it had more than twelve hours to get where they want. The faster you chase after them, the more they'll be waiting on you."

"Is that a fact?" Kessler said in a sarcastic tone. "Marshal, with all due respect, I don't think you know Coy Dallas or the men in his gang. Jefferson Tanner, a ruthless killer in his own right is a former Confederate who rode with Quantrill when he was sixteen. The man loves gunning down people. There's good evidence he's recruited Harold Hixson and Floyd Morton, two former federal prisoners from Nebraska, paroled after five years for railroad payroll robbery. Hoofprints we've found show they're riding with two others as yet unknown. But Dallas is in charge, have no doubt. And he will not stop until he's avenged his sentence. The faster we find him, the safer the territory."

The detective's plan wasn't a bad one, but Cole saw an advantage in staying put. "I can't say I know this fellow as well as you, Mr. Keesler. But if I was him, I'd figure there'd be people just like us right on his heels." He pointed to the bodies. "He ain't exactly going about this without trying to bring notice. I think he's counting on someone like yourself following him real close. Kind of like a bear I hunted once. Tracked it for three days, until one morning I came upon a hill to find it behind me. Had I not a Sharpe's rifle, I'd ended up as just the glow in its coat. That bear was a wild animal, too."

"Your point is taken, Marshal," said Keesler, who arched his thumb to the west as an order to his men to ride in the direction. "But I'll stay with proven tactics. I was part of the original party that caught Dallas. I'm certain the same procedure will catch him again."

The pack of Pinkertons kicked at their mounts' flanks. Cole watched them as they soon crested the far hill. He faced about to Richard, who sat confused atop the sorrel, then pointed at the two bodies.

"There they are. You want to aim that camera on them?" Richard cowered away from the question. "Then what are you waiting for? Go ride to their barn and fetch two shovels."

CHAPTER EIGHT

As dusk settled into night, Cole patted down the dual mounds of dirt. He leaned back, listening to the crack of his sore bones at the base of his spine. The work was tiring, but necessary if he wanted to keep a clear conscience for the remainder of the journey.

Richard approached from behind with two small crosses hammered out from scrap lumber found in the barn. Neither of them held a firm angle, but they appeared sturdy enough to stay in place during the stout winds. Without orders, the young man placed a cross at the head of each mound while Cole slammed the top with the back of the shovel. Once the markers were standing upright, both men removed their hats at the same time, eyeing each other for the next propriety.

"Go ahead and say something," Cole said.

"Me?" Richard's surprise passed with the

weight of duty. He took a deep breath and rolled his eyes to the dim sky. "Heavenly Father, please accept this man and woman into your heavenly bounds. Amen."

The few words forced open one of Cole's eyes. "That's it?"

"Well, if you feel there's need to say more, be my guest."

Richard's tone perturbed Cole more than the simple eulogy. "Ain't you going to say nothing about what kind of folks they were?"

"I didn't know them. How am I to say something about them?"

"You could see they were good folks," Cole said, pointing to the house. "You can't just say 'Dear Father, welcome them into Heaven.' "

"I thought it satisfactory, but if you think it lacking, I eagerly await your rendition."

The dare stopped Cole. He put on his hat and pulled the shovel's spade from the ground. "You're the writer. I was expecting better." He tossed the tool in the grass and mounted his horse to ride to the house. After the short distance, he entered the front door and retrieved the lantern. A match to the wick illuminated the hollow home.

He went right to the cupboard next to the stove, not wanting to poke around any further among the Palmers' remnants. He opened the cupboard to find two sacks of ground flour behind three metal pots of various sizes. One last jar of peeled pear slices hid in the corner. He removed the flour and the jar. Seeing no other sign of food, he went to a chest next to the wall hoping to find more supplies stored. He raised the lid to find clothes, figurines of childhood fancy, and aged tintypes of older men and women seated in a parlor, but there was no food.

"Now we're ransacking the place?"

At Richard's voice, Cole turned toward the door and lifted the lantern to illuminate the young man's face. "I was just looking for more food for the trip. It ain't like they're going to eat it."

The response was calm and low toned, and it nagged worse than a whiny kitten. "So did you find any?"

Cole peered down at the contents of the chest and spoke in a voice of relent. "No." Richard slowly came to his side and inspected the chest. Cole felt obliged to say what he thought. "Appears to be the keepsakes of a family. One that had a child."

"What are you saying?"

After a long inhaled breath, Cole dug the sleeve from his pocket. "There's another woman that we haven't found yet. A young one, maybe as old as fifteen or sixteen, but not yet a growed woman, is my guess by the length of this."

Richard took the torn cloth. "You think Dallas's gang kidnapped her?"

Cole nodded and let the lid slam shut. "A little fun as they go from one place to the next." He stepped to the right, lifting the lantern to shine into the dark interior. "I don't know if we're going to find much to use of what's left in here."

"Maybe we should have gone with the Pinkertons."

"Maybe," Cole said with a shrug. "I doubt them fellows are concerned about who Dallas is going to harm next. But too late now. We'd just get lost in the dark."

After they found a suitable spot to rest without disturbing too much, Richard wouldn't let Cole rest. "Why did you lie to those men about your name?"

"Because," he answered while he settled on the floor, "I didn't want them to know my real one." He took his knife and cut through the wax seal of the jar of pears.

"That's obvious." Richard came closer to the light, and after a few moments, sat next to the grounded lantern. "You didn't want them to arrest you, did you?"

Cole shook his head while he unfastened the top of the jar and stabbed one of the pear halves. "Nope. Didn't fear them arresting me. It was a bullet in the back I was trying to keep from." With the blade stuck between his teeth, he bit off the fruit and chewed. The soft texture had a fermented taste. "Pinkertons ain't like real law. They're a business. Might look good if they was to bring in a man with a reputation with a gun. Wouldn't matter if that man had anything to do with what they were out there for. Kind of like hunting for deer. If you can't find no deer, and a couple of jackrabbits come along, you shoot them instead. When you come back home, it appears you did something useful."

Richard broke a grin. "I hesitate to say, but I do see your point." He gazed at the dark surroundings. "So where do we go from here?"

"I don't know." The simple question went beyond the boundaries of the present in Cole's head. "Ever been to San Francisco?"

"Why?" Richard's brow creased in the center. "Do you think they're headed that way?"

"No. I was just wondering if you know what it's like there. I never been to California."

"I cannot claim to, either. It's a very modern place, so I've read." He stammered out facts. "Numerous tall buildings, both educated men and women, a good deal of culture there, opera houses and the like. In some sense, you could call it a rival of New York City, Philadelphia, Boston, or the other large cities in the East." Once it seemed that was all the reporter knew about the city, his tone changed back to his nosy standard. "Why would you ask such a question in light of the circumstance?"

Again Cole shrugged, then wagged his finger. "You been to the opera house? I mean the one back in Copper Springs?"

Richard's brow curled once more. "You're asking about that woman, aren't you? Vivien Hooper?"

That nip was a little too close to the bone. "No," he answered, sticking another pear half on his tongue, then pushing the jar in front of Richard. "Why would you be asking that?"

"Because," the young man replied as he carefully examined the fruit, just as a cat would a mouse after killing it, "I see it in your eyes."

"My eyes?"

"Yes." Richard took the Bowie knife and jabbed at a pear half unsuccessfully. "I'm not blind, Clay. She's a beautiful woman. It was hard not to notice how your eyes lit up when you spoke about her." Another stab still produced no bounty.

"When did I talk about her?"

Richard looked to Cole in frustration. "Just now."

The remark got Cole's goat. He snatched the knife from Richard while sliding the jar between his legs. He plunged the point deep into a pear half and held up the captured morsel in front of his young friend. "I never said nothing about her," he said, then bit the half and chewed it.

After having been embarrassed by his lack of technique, Richard reclaimed the knife and jar. "If she means nothing to you, then why are you so adamant about denying it?" The question stopped Cole long enough for Richard to stab one of the last three halves.

"Because it ain't true."

"Now you sound like a schoolgirl. The more front you show, the greater you confirm the accusation."

The mess of long words only confused Cole. As he watched Richard master the knife, he thought of the truth of what he had said. What if he was right? The red-haired woman did have a plain way of pursuing what she wanted that got his blood to boiling. The last time a woman went after him that strong was near ten years ago.

It was the dark-haired Polly who first tamed him. And she knew right where his leash was hid. It wasn't just the meshing as man and woman that pulled his heart then. Although she took money from other men to share a bed for the hour, he saw something different in her from the rest of the women, and she in him. She had no kin, no man hauling her from one town to the next, and no one to listen to after the last of her customers had passed out.

They were two of kind. A pair of tortured souls alone in the world who sought something better than what they had and what was ahead of the next bend. It was the mutual misery they shared in common, and their comfort of each other with the hope of survival. Maybe that reason made it so easy to decide to settle together. After weeks of living each day under the same roof and sleeping under the same blanket, nothing gave him greater sense of a better future than news he'd swelled her belly with a baby. Polly never looked happier.

He inhaled to slow his racing heart and closed his eyes. The memory of the damage of a careless flame still burned at the scar in his soul. A few more long breaths settled his mind. He squelched the visions from his memory. There would be no more thoughts of women for now. He couldn't afford to tread so near.

When he focused on Richard, the last pear half still dodged the point of the knife. "You going to eat them all?"

A shroud of surprise and shame came over the young reporter's face. "I thought you offered the rest to me. I was hungry. All I'd eaten was that rotted bacon from last night."

"No matter," Cole said, reclining on the wood floor. "Go ahead. Take it. I'm done."

In a show of remorse, Richard replaced the jar's lid and pulled the clamp tight over it. A moment went by before he garnered the courage to speak. "So what do we do tomorrow?"

"Pick up the trail where we left it."

A huff from Richard broke the silence. "You surprise me, Clay. I thought we were after the men who took your friend. I would have thought you would be in more of a hurry to find him."

Cole couldn't argue. There was another sad realization that took his mind. "I don't know about Choate. I admit, when I first thought they had him, I wanted to find him. Find him quick. To save him. But the more I see what these fellows done, the little I'm thinking he's still alive." He put his hat over his face.

"And what about this young woman they have? The one you think lived in this very house?"

The truth was too much work to hide. "I don't give much for her chances, neither. Traveling with a female ain't the same as a man. They can't keep up, don't take to the sun during the day or the cold at night. That ain't to say that they ain't making her do work for them along with having their way with her. After they'd have their fill of her, or maybe she of them, my guess is that if the nature of Montana don't wear her down to a nub . . ." He paused to think of a better end for the girl, but the honest prediction was too large to swallow back. "Well, I think they'll kill her."

He waited for an argument of hope from Richard, but none came. Although the floor was hard, his bones relaxed on the flat, even wood. Thoughts of turning about entered his head, but it was too late in the evening to give much attention to them. Perhaps in the morning his head would be clearer, as well as his sense for where the men he sought would head next. For now, rest wasn't the worst idea.

"Blow out the lantern."

CHAPTER NINE

With the sun already burning bright, Cole hurried to pack what supplies he could stuff onto the bay he found tethered behind the house. The lost time nagged the back of his mind. It had been a stretch of years before he didn't rise before dawn. Now it appeared the short time on a soft bunk in the Copper Springs jail had spoiled him like a child with no chores.

"How long do you think it will take to get to the next home on the map?"

"We ain't going there."

Richard's jaw dropped as low as his eyes went wide. "What?"

Cole continued to tie down the hank strings of the packs. "I've been thinking. With another late start, chance of us getting to another spread that far away in time for stopping Dallas from killing more people ain't likely. Don't like agreeing with him, but that Keesler fellow was right. All we're going to do is dig more graves going about it this way."

"How do you propose to pursue Dallas and his gang?"

Cole motioned for Richard to pick another sack of flour.

"One thing we know for sure is some or all of that gang was right here." Once finished securing the last pack, he turned to Richard. "We're going to track him. Now, get on your horse."

The order took a moment to sink through. However, once it did, the reporter didn't waste any time climbing into the saddle. He turned the sorrel and was prepared to kick to a gallop until Cole held up a hand.

"We ain't going to see nothing by scampering out of here." He nudged the palomino and went down the path they had gone the previous day. The bay was tied to Richard's mount. As they passed the graves, Richard removed his hat, but Cole dismounted.

"Is something out of place?"

"Looking for something."

"What?"

He shrugged. "Ain't found it yet." Knees on the ground, he crawled through the grass around where the bodies once lay. He needed a breath to concentrate on finding what he was after and ignore the murder that took place at this spot. He swatted the tall stems from side to side, moving farther and farther away from the graves.

"Should I help?"

"No," Cole said firmly. "You just stay where you are. I don't need you traipsing about, muddling up what I'm looking for."

"And what is that?"

He exhaled in frustration. "Something I can follow." With more swats of grass, he crawled farther, driven by the gut feeling that a sign would give him a guess where to go next.

"I see something."

The announcement stopped the swatting of grass and turned Cole about. "What?"

Richard, still on the saddle, pointed a few feet in front of the horse he rode. "Right there."

Cole stood and walked to where the finger directed. Only dirt and grass were in view. "I don't see nothing."

"Right there." Richard came off the horse, one hand holding the reins as he pointed with the other. "It appears to be mud."

Because Cole had not sighted the discovery, the revelation of finding mud in the Montana high country drooped his shoulders. His mood changed when the reporter knelt next to a flattened clod. "It's a different color than the rest."

Cole bent next to it and agreed with a nod. "Part sand. Not plowed soil like around here." That interested him more than the color.

"You see. I was right. Maybe you should listen to me more often."

"I just might do that," he replied, carefully lifting the piece of earth. An indent caught his eye. "This is from a horse. That mark is a spur in the metal shoe that weren't filed off. If this dust did come from someplace not around here, we might be looking for that mark among the tracks we come across." He rose off the ground and bobbed his head forward. "Come on. Let's go."

Following the angle where the print was left, Cole gambled that it was flung from the hoof of a horse being ridden in a hurry. They climbed over the hill and went northwest. At better than an amble, they covered ridge after ridge, stopping occasionally to survey the ground for more tracks. None of the ones found matched the one he was after.

The sound of water lapping against rocks crept into his ear. He knew he was close when the scent of the river whirled into the breeze. Once over a small rise, he pulled up on the palomino and stared down. In a few minutes, Richard came alongside.

"At last, water," said the reporter. "What river is this?"

"Missouri." Cole stared upriver and down, looking for a favorable spot at which to cross. Without one coming into immediate view and with a spit in the middle from where he was, he figured the low level was an invitation. "Have you ever crossed a river this size?"

Richard shook his head with eyes noticeably wider than when he had arrived at the spot.

"Keep a tight hold on them reins, yours and the bay's. We can't afford to lose nothing at where we're at and where we're headed." Cole nudged the palomino to the edge of the shore. Once the blond mount hesitated, he smacked the rump to force it into the water. In two steps, the surface swallowed horse and rider neck high to just below the bridle. Cole leaned forward, the chill soothing his scorched body for only a minute at most, then numbing his legs. He kept the palomino swimming into the current, all the while maintaining a grip on the saddle horn. Finally, hooves hit the muddy shore and he rode out of the river.

He twisted about. Richard remained on

the other side. Cole waved. "What you waiting on?"

The reporter pointed at the camera. "I can't risk ruining it." Richard dismounted and after more than a minute had his equipment loose from the horse. Cole glanced at the sun. They were losing too much time.

After three failed attempts to do so, Richard mounted the sorrel with the tripod legs slung over his shoulder. When Cole saw two sets of reins in the same hand, he knew it would be trouble. Before he could yell to correct the mistake, Richard had kicked the horse to charge into the water.

The current quickly pushed horse and rider downriver. "Steer into it!" Despite Cole's yell, the reporter couldn't control his horse long enough before the bay's reins slipped through his hands. Fearful of losing the supplies, Cole kicked the palomino back into the water. The bay made better progress to stay in a straight line. Soon he was able to grasp the reins, turn the palomino about, and get both horses back to the shore. Richard didn't enjoy the same ease.

With greater concern paid to the security of the camera, the tinhorn had lost control of his mount midway through the swift water. The sorrel wanted to return to the original side. Richard yanked the reins the

160

other way. Cole released the bay's reins and once again set into the river after Richard. With the horse's hooves splashing, Cole rode along the shoreline to set the palomino on a course to catch the sorrel as it drifted down the river.

As Richard and his horse came close, Cole had the palomino into the water, reins in one hand, his right palm open to snatch the bridle. With the leather straps finally in hand, he nudged the palomino back to the shore. When both horses, both riders, and one camera were out of the river, Cole let loose the bridle.

"You damn fool. Nearly get yourself killed for that!"

Still heaving wind in and out, Richard looked at Cole, then the camera, as if to imply his life mattered no more than the stick-legged box. Water dripped a steady stream from his shoes. Cole turned his horse around and shook his head in disgust.

As the day wore on, they crossed a few milder streams without trouble. Richard didn't have the courage to come near him. Cole kept his eyes front, concentrating on the prairie and distant ranges before them. As he did, two figures slowly emerged.

Cole slowed the palomino. It wasn't long before Richard came next to him. "Do you know who that is?" he asked Cole.

While keeping his eyes on the approaching riders, Cole shook his head. "Not for sure." As the pair came near, riding side by side, the figures presented familiar poses. One wore a brown hat with a high crown, and wool coat with numerous bright stripes, as though it was made from a blanket. The other wore on his head only the braids symbolic of his tribe. His coat wasn't as thick and the colors were faded, no doubt bleached from years in the sun.

"Blackfeet," said Cole. When the strangers slowed their horses in front of them, Richard looked to the men's animal-skin boots, then at Cole, as if confused.

Uncertain of their language, Cole nodded at them when they arrived and opened his coat slowly to reveal his badge. The one with the hat released reins and held up his hands, circling his fingers, then straightening in different patterns. Long ago, Cole had learned the signs of the tribes in the territory.

"I think they found something." He inhaled and let it out in a pained huff. "I think he's telling me it's a woman." The one in the hat put his palm to his cheek and pointed at Cole. "She's a white woman." Cole pointed two fingers at his own eyes, then pointed to the open land. The one in the hat nodded and turned about.

"What are they doing? Did you get them to leave?"

"No. This is their land. I told them to take us to where she is." Cole followed the natives. Richard wasn't far behind.

After riding through high grass for several miles, they finally stopped. Neither of the strangers left the backs of the horses. Cole dismounted and went through the grass. At first, he saw a boulder cut out of a small arroyo. Next, he noticed ashes of a fire that was all cold to the touch. Small discolored clumps of dirt surrounded the bare ground around the fire. He dabbed one with his finger and put it to the end of his tongue. It was blood, but not as much from a bullet wound. When he rose to stand, he saw white filtering through the yellow and green grass.

Taking in another long breath, he took steps that put him over the body of a young blond-haired girl. Blood from the bullet hole in the center of her bare chest was dry. He closed his eyes for only an instant, then focused on the colors and pattern of the dress. He drew the cloth from his pocket, then looked to the torn sleeve of the dress. They were the same.

Sadness from the loss of such a young life made him turn his head. Her shredded clothes left little doubt as to what had happened to her before she was killed. Anger swelled inside him, but he pushed it back down his gut and went to the two natives. With arm and hand signals he asked for them to care for the girl's body. Their answer disappointed him. He watched the one in the hat motion through another story. It disturbed him more. Finally, he asked one last favor. When they responded, he went to Richard.

"If my guess is right, they're saying they spotted a group of men riding through here yesterday."

"Do you think they were the ones that did this?" Richard asked in a whisper.

Cole shrugged. "Don't seem that way. I think this was done longer ago than that. But could be." He glanced at the Blackfeet pair. "I asked them to bury her, but they said they didn't want lost white spirits wandering their land. So I asked if they'd take her to their settlement so she can be taken by the Indian Affairs people. They said *we* can take her. But it doesn't appear to be too far." He looked back at Richard. "We'll have to put more supplies on our horses to fit her on the bay."

They made the Blackfeet settlement by

nightfall. Cole tried to give care to the girl's body. The tribe gave him a blanket to wrap her with, mainly to keep the soul warm and not seek their shelter. Spent from the day's ride, he and Richard were given a meal and a fire to sleep by.

By daybreak, Cole had rousted Richard once more and expressed his appreciation to the tribe. They packed their gear and saddled the mounts for another long day. If there were tracks, he wanted to find them as soon as possible. The fresher the better.

Coy Dallas rode up the steep hill. Tanner stopped his walk with an armload of branches. "They ain't but two or three miles away. You sure that thing can do the job?"

Tanner smiled at the question. "You seen it."

Dallas nodded without a smile. "I seen too much go wrong. I'll leave you Hix, like you asked. But I'm taking the rest north. We'll meet up at the line shack. You remember?" Tanner nodded. "Well, be sure to tell Hix case you two get separated." About to kick his horse for the trip north, he held the reins to bark one last time. "Make sure it's done quick. We can't have any more going wrong." He spurred the flanks before he heard the reply.

At midday, thirst slowed him. Cole dismounted and pulled his canteen. Richard soon followed. "Thank God. I was wondering when we would stop to eat."

"We ain't stopping." He opened the canteen and cupped his hand to hold the water under the palomino's nose. "Water your horse. Make sure he gets more than you."

Met with a snarled lip, Richard complied. "Well, when do we stop? We must have traveled ten miles."

"More like five." Cole looked to the vast plain between him and the tall mountains barely over the horizon. "But we're making better time than yesterday. I think we might make them hills before sundown."

"My Lord," Richard spoke with awe. "Those? It'll take a week at least to get there."

The estimate amused Cole. Refilling his hand with water, he let the horse lick some, then wiped his face with the slick palm. The few drops spilling to the ground drew his attention. "Only if you don't slow —" A horseshoe print in the dust stopped his thoughts. He knelt next to it. The angle now pointed almost due north. He crouched closer. The dust was loose, but the print was all intact. The flawed spur mark was well defined. "Mount up," he said, capping the canteen.

"But I thought we were going to rest the horses."

Cole stepped into the stirrup and climbed into the saddle. "That was before I saw what we've been chasing." He pointed to the print. "It was left there within the day." He motioned toward the terrain to the north. "Must be following a different lead than what I figured." He nudged the palomino in the direction. The sorrel and bay weren't long behind.

The track was encouraging but confusing. The fresh print meant whoever it belonged to wasn't far ahead. When he began, he thought at least three days separated him from those he sought. As he neared the first of the ridgetops, his own words came back into his head. Maybe they decided to not flee. The notion had him release his right hand from the reins and rest it on the butt of his Colt.

As they came over the edge of the hill, the sight of riders sent his heart racing and he reined in. Their attention was turned away from him, but should they face about they'd have him dead in the saddle. He glanced to the side. No cover would protect him.

Again, he looked to them, but familiar shapes calmed his chest. The men on top of the hill wore bowler hats.

"Those are the Pinkerton men," said Richard as he came alongside. Cole couldn't speak, chiding himself inside for being such a fool. For the entire day, he'd been chasing something he wasn't looking to find. He glared at Richard. It was the tinhorn's discovery that had sent them on this fool chase. But it was he that gave it spit. Once he saw a few of the men turn their horses around at them, there was no sneaking away.

Cole and Richard kicked at the flanks to hurry their horses up the hill. Keesler held his mount steady with one hand on the reins at the top of one rise while holding a spyglass with the other. Cole slowed the palomino to come alongside the leader of the Pinkerton agents. He noticed the direction Keesler aimed the spyglass, at first thinking maybe he was right all along and one of the Dallas gang had been spotted. However, when Cole squinted into the distance, all he saw was the familiar profile of grazing buffalo.

"I don't think them's what we're after."

Keesler pulled his eye from the glass only long enough to recognize Cole. "Good morning, Marshal Hayes. I wasn't sure you'd be joining us today."

"I see you didn't get very far without us."

He resumed looking through the glass. "Magnificent creatures," he muttered. "But just as destructive as the savages that feed off them."

Cole breathed heavy, remembering his own days some ten years before, slaughtering the animals on orders for the Army. "There ain't many left these days," he murmured in regret. "Those that are left here belong to the Blackfeet by treaty."

Keesler lowered the spyglass, gave a smirk at Cole, then collapsed the small scope to hand to him to see. One of his hired guns handed Keesler a bolt-action rifle. He opened the action, loading the chamber, then slammed it closed to fire. "I don't think they'll mind missing one, do you?"

The disregard stung like a slap across the face. Cole peered around at the Pinkerton agents to be sure his next move wouldn't get him killed. Their pistols and rifles were at rest, so he gave Richard a bob of the head to retreat out of a line of fire. Keesler raised the rifle to the shoulder. Cole drew the Colt revolver, poking the muzzle at Keesler's temple.

"Disrespecting the law is a jailing offense. Disrespecting me is a death sentence."

When the leader of the detectives drooped the rifle's aim and edged his face around to his startled followers, Cole pulled the hammer back.

"Easy, Marshal. We're all friends here. All working together."

He had done the worst. Feelings wouldn't be the same now. "Let's set affairs straight. I ain't your friend. And I have to say that we stopped working together as soon as you aimed that rifle." He peeked around and saw five itchy fingers ready to take up for one of their own. Trying to get away from that many men would require spraying a heap of lead over a long stretch over open country. "So this is how it is going to be from now on. I give the orders. No one is doing any shooting until I give an order. And that includes killing any buffalo just for sport. Anybody here can't abide that, best pack your iron and head south."

"Don't be an idiot. We aren't going to leave."

Cole pushed the muzzle firmer. "This ain't up to a vote. If your men don't agree to it, you will never learn of it." Cole scanned left and right. All of the men seemed bewildered as to what to do next. "Do as I say!" His booming command forced the five shooters to comply. Pistols were shoved into holsters and tucked into gunbelts. Rifles slid into scabbards. "That includes you, Mr. Keesler." With only minor hesitation, their leader tossed away the bolt-action rifle. "Now, the rest of you move forward."

It took only moments before the men nudged their horses, passing Cole and Keesler. Richard held the sorrel and bay in place at the rear. Once all the men were ahead, Cole rested the Colt's hammer and cautiously pulled the muzzle away from Keesler's head, but he didn't holster the weapon. Keesler, once he was able to turn his face in full range, glared at Cole with eyes wide.

"You'll pay for that. No one puts a gun to my head, Marshal Hayes. You may have a badge to hide behind. But there will come a day when we will settle all accounts. Whether you're wearing that badge or not."

The threat was amusing. "I'll make it simple for you, Mr. Keesler. Once this business is over chasing after Dallas, then just you and me can settle whatever you wish. But until it's over, should I smell a hint you come to starting our little feud one minute before Dallas is dead or behind bars, then I'll kill you right where you stand. Now, join your men."

With a last sneer, Keesler kicked his mount to a gallop to make up the distance. Cole was in no hurry to ride along. He kept the pistol handy in his grip as Richard rode next to him.

"I think you made your point."

He angled a glance at the young man. "Well," he drawled, "let's see what kind of fight I stirred up. May not have been the best thing to pick a fight with them Pinkertons." He nudged the palomino down the slope he'd sent the detectives. At the bottom lay a dry gully with a high bank on the far side. "Just the same, you'll be needing to watch these fellows from now on. Tin star or no, once a man's been shamed in front of his men, likely as not he'll be looking for a reason to put himself back on top."

"What do you think he'll do?"

"Hard to say. But you'll need to be watching. When we're around these fellows, we'll need to be looking for where their weapons are. How close they keep them when they're in camp. Just when you're believing they're your friends, that's when you need fear them worst."

They watched the agents huddle closer halfway down the slope. Cole regripped the pistol, edging his finger into the trigger guard, and stopped the palomino. "This don't look good."

"What do think they're talking about?"

"How they're going to get the drop on us." After a few moments, the pack began slowly moving farther down the slope, but Cole kept the palomino at a stand.

Richard did the same. "How long are we going to stay here?"

"Ah, we'll let them get a little further up ahead. Give them time to stew a little longer. Maybe let them simmer down."

Richard nodded. "Sounds good to me. Anything that avoids further trouble." He pointed to the top of the ridge at a clump of greenery. "Maybe let them get to that small tree?"

The comment drew Cole's attention. He stared at the unusual form. At a distance he gauged to be more than five hundred yards up a considerable incline, the crown of the bush appeared at an angle, as if the limbs were growing toward the ground. With a quick glance about he noticed no growth other than the tall grass. He squinted hard. With the spyglass still in his hand, he extended the sections and put it to his eye. The growth's density didn't seem normal. The longer he concentrated, the more a noticeable shape appeared. A spoked wheel.

Shadows moved through the limbs.

"That ain't no tree."

Cole slapped the spyglass small and kicked the palomino. Loud bursts came from atop the ridge. White smoke billowed like a cloud from the spot of the bush. Clumps of dirt popped into air all around the Pinkertons.

"The gully," Cole shouted at Richard.

Bullets pelted the ground at a rapid mechanical rate. Only one weapon could do that.

Streams of gunfire strafed across the detectives, blowing bloody holes into one agent and his mount, dropping the bodies in a heap. Cole rode past without glancing back and kept his eyes aimed at the gully. With Keesler in the lead, the Pinkertons rode in scattered formation toward the safety of the tall bank.

Lead slugs ripped apart the ground in front of a galloping horse. It reared and bucked, throwing its rider to the dirt, then scampered back up the slope. Panicked and defiant, the hired detective drew his revolver and fired blindly up the hill. He got off two rounds before three tore open his chest and blew him backward with the force of a gale.

By the time Cole neared the tall bank, Keesler and the remaining three men had taken cover behind the bank. Cole didn't want to risk dismounting and be afoot, so he pulled the reins hard over, bringing the palomino's muzzle high on the left, sending the animal to fall on its right side while he jumped off the saddle. Richard quickly followed, but his attempt to duplicate the feat resulted in his flying off the saddle to crash against the embankment.

Cole looked to him while still holding the palomino's reins tight. "Are you hit?"

"I'm alive," Richard answered in a stammer.

More lead pummeled the high edge of the bank. Dirt rained down on them from the shots. Keesler and his men rose to fire single shots from their pistols, then ducked down.

"Save your lead," Cole cried. "He's out of range. That's a Gatling up there!"

Whether or not they could hear him over the chaos of bullets ricocheting by or the ring of their own shots, the agents continued their futile return fire.

"You can't hit him. He's out of range."

The Pinkertons didn't stop firing and began reloading. Once the first of them had rearmed his revolver, he stood up and carefully aimed the gun at arm's length. Before he squeezed off the shot, a bullet split his head open from front to back.

Cole turned his eyes away from the scene. He sighted the Mouton rifle in the scabbard. A voice from the past crept into his mind. He drew the rifle and scrambled for the ammunition pouch in the saddlebag.

"What are you doing?" Richard's squeaky question didn't deter Cole from finding the pouch and drawing a single loaded magazine.

"I'm going to end this with the only thing that can shoot back." He pulled back the loading bolt and inserted the shell-filled casing. Anguished cries came from the right. He glanced that way to see the last of Keesler's men writhe on the ground, hands across his bleeding belly.

Cole pumped the action, but hesitated as bullets whisked past.

"What are you going to do?"

He glanced at Richard. "I'm waiting for him to have to change out the cartridge feeder." More bullets pounded the dirt and grass. Like the waves of a river ebbing against the shore, slugs tore a line in the dirt from over Cole's head to the right toward the cowering Keesler.

A moment of calm gave Cole the gumption to act. He let go of the reins, rose, and steadied the barrel at the white smoke. The slight breeze took it away. In sight stood the two-wheel Gatling gun with the tall figure standing behind it. Cole fired. The booming blast sent fire out of the muzzle. Sparks flew off the Gatling barrels from the ricochet. The shooter appeared spooked that a shot had actually reached that far. Cole pumped the action again. A gunshot rang out from the right again. A peek there showed Keesler standing exposed over the bank and shooting a pistol while swearing up a storm. The Gatling turned his way.

"No!" shouted Cole. The Gatling's barrel turned, popping off three shots. With the weapon aimed away from him, Cole squinted an eye and lined up the shooter in the sights and fired. Recoil stunted the speed of pumping the action, but once that was done, he aimed again — only to see his target lying on the ground.

Instinct wanted him to shrink back behind the protective embankment, but the silence froze him in place. The Gatling gun stood unattended, like a tamed beast waiting for its master's next demand. But there was no hand on the crank.

He looked left. Keesler lay prone on the edge of the embankment, arms sprawled away from his side, eyes wide open to sparkle in the afternoon light, blood spilling out of the bowler on his head like a freshly tapped keg.

Another sure glance confirmed that the

Gatling was no longer a threat. He lowered the Mouton rifle and peered down at the knee-cradling Richard. "You still alive?"

With jumpy and jerky motion, the young reporter inspected his legs, arms, and chest. Once sure, he looked again at Cole and nodded. "Are they gone?"

"One's dead. Don't know if there's more." He looked right again at the Pinkerton bodies and shook his head. "Damn fools," he muttered.

"What is that thing?"

The curious question brought Cole's attention to where Richard pointed at the Mouton rifle and reflected. More than a year had passed since he met with the foreigner named Serge Mouton while hunting for hidden Indian gold with an English dandy and another shapely redhead in Texas. The man bragged in his slurred cut of words about how the rifle he invented was the "savior of mankind." The boast touted that the weapon was so powerful and accurate, so easy to fire, and used magazines with long rifle cartridges for rapid reloading, that to attempt to challenge an army equipped with such rifles would be folly. It was the same purpose of the Gatling gun during the War Between the States. However, Mouton explained in his brash tone that the Gatling gun was an artillery piece and unable to compete with his design of a mobile weapon every soldier carried. Later, it became clear that Mouton, a servant to the French, had eyes on helping Mexican revolutionary Francisco Guru arm renegade Comanches with the rifles to root out Texans from Texas. When the plan failed, the thieves turned on each other and forced Cole and Mouton to a knife fight to the death. The scar in his belly wasn't as fatal as the one he had made in the cocky foreigner's throat. Yet the only true brag that man ever made was the ability of his invention.

Cole again looked at Richard. "It's a long story."

"Help me" came as a weak cry from the right. Cole went to the kid with the belly wound, who lay prostrate on his back, and knelt next to him, still wary of the Gatling gun on the high ground.

He pried the young man's hands from his bloody shirt. The cloth oozed blood like a sieve. Cole ripped the shirt to get a better look. The motion brought a loud scream from the wounded man. The bullet hole was as big as a dollar. "Ain't nothing I can do for you, son. You're gut-shot. There's no fixing what that slug has tore up inside."

"Please, Marshal," he stuttered. "I don't

want to die. I'm only twenty-three. I ain't supposed to die at my age. Please, don't let me die."

Richard's shadow edged over the young kid's face. "Isn't there something we can do for him?"

"Nah," Cole replied in a hushed breath. "You know how far it is to a town. If we found one, ain't for sure there's a doc there that can fix this. Just putting him on a horse would be like setting fire to his insides." He looked to the kid. "You fellows have any whiskey? Spirits of any kind to wash the wound with? Ease your pain?"

The kid could only rock his head from side to side. "Mr. Keesler wouldn't let us have no drinks while on duty." The words gave the kid pain, so he sucked in air through his teeth. Cole had seen this before. His own pa died this way from the last minié ball fired in the war. A shot he caused to be fired. He closed his eyes to clear the memory from his mind. It wasn't a time to be recalling his own past. Yet he knew what was to come.

"It may take days for you to die, son. If that slug didn't cut into nothing that makes you breathe, it sure tore into your guts, swashing your own mess around inside you to swell up everything it touches."

"No, no," came another plea, but Cole could only shake his head.

"Clay," Richard said in an admonishing tone, "give him some dignity, at least."

Cole turned his shaking head to Richard. "Ain't no dignity about it. What's done or said, the end will come no matter." He let the air from his chest seep out and hung his head. More time would be wasted nursing the kid in vain. With another long breath in and out, Cole took the kid's arm and stripped away the sleeve. Before he heard a complaint, he drew the Bowie knife and sliced through the vessels in the wrist. Blood shot in the air. He turned the wrist down to dirt. The kid's eyes went wide but didn't jerk from the cut, revealing that he had no pain greater than his belly wound.

"What have you done?"

Cole rose, turned his back, and replaced the knife in the sheath. "Get away from him."

Richard came at a charge next to him and grabbed his shoulder. "I said, what have you done?"

More tugs at the shoulder got Cole's goat. He snatched Richard at the collar, pulling the reporter's face within inches of his own. "What had to be." He shoved Richard to the ground and went to retrieve the palomino, but stopped for only a moment. "You want to see him squeezed with pain till nightfall? This way, he'll be gone in an hour or less." He needed to relieve his own conscience. "I ain't the cause of what's going to happen to him. I just hurried the result."

He gave only a glance up the hill to the stoic monster on wheels. It had done all this. None of the bloodshed was of his doing or choosing. Nevertheless, he was the one left to deal with the remains.

He saw a shiny chrome Remington short-barreled revolver lying in the grass. He picked it up, recognized the .36-caliber, then searched the pockets of the corpse with the skull split in half. "No sense leaving still-good ammunition and firearms behind," he said aloud, mostly to himself. He found a box of cartridges and tucked those in his coat. Next, he returned to the boy he'd just sent on his way to Heaven. The kid's eyes were stuck open in a blind death stare, although his chest still billowed breath slightly. Cole glimpsed Richard, still sitting on the grass, head hung in despair. Lying beside the body was a Smith & Wesson Schofield .45 pistol. He picked it off the grass and opened the breech. Six unfired shells filled the cylinders. He shook his head at the shame of the young kid dying without getting off a shot, then snapped the breech shut and tossed the weapon to Richard. "Time's come for you to learn to use that." He held up the .36. "This will hurt a fellow bad. But if not aimed dead center, it may only make him mad." He pointed at the .45. "That will kill a fellow dead most any place you hit him." He motioned toward the body on the ground. "See if he has any more shells in his pockets."

Once he had the Mouton rifle in hand, he went the short distance to where his horse had gone to escape the barrage. It wasn't long before he mounted and was able to catch the skittish sorrel, but the bay with all the supplies couldn't be seen. He looked to the top of the incline where the Gatling stood. It had proved to be the best vantage point of the whole valley. He rode, leading the sorrel by the reins to where Richard still sat on the ground.

"We need to find our supplies."

It took a longer-than-needed moment for Richard to angle his eyes to Cole. "We're leaving?" He gazed at the dead bodies surrounding him. "What about these men? Aren't we going to bury them?"

Cole shook his head. "Ain't got time."

Again Richard rose to a take a defiant

stance. "What? We made time for that farmer and his wife."

"That was two holes. It could take most of tomorrow to dig six." He held out the sorrel's reins for Richard to take. When the reporter relented and took them, Cole looked at the bodies, then at the top of the hill. "When we get to a town, we'll tell the local law there what happened. They can send out the church folk that will see these men buried." He pointed at Keesler when Richard took the saddle. "That's the way he would want it. Remember?"

Cole turned the palomino, found where the embankment was shallow, and lashed the reins against the flanks to charge up the hill. The incline was so sharp, he leaned over the horn to keep his balance over the long grade. More than once he needed to kick the mount to get to the top. Richard was slow in driving the sorrel over the same ground. A glance behind showed the camera legs stabbing the horse's hindquarters.

While he waited, he dismounted and went to the Gatling gun. The body lying behind it was tall. By the amount of blood splashed across the shirt and duster, a bullet had gone through the chest and right into the heart. The Mouton rifle had proved itself. He didn't recognize this shooter, but his long blond hair resembled another fool who loved battle, George A. Custer. He stood to see a stray mount grazing in the distance, but it wasn't the bay. He scanned the valley below and didn't see the pack animal with all the food. When he looked closer to the ground near the Gatling, he saw another set of hoofprints. They showed the flawed mark on one shoe. He stared into the distance but saw no sign of the other shooter.

With whinnies of agitation, the sorrel struggled up to the crest of the hill. Richard gripped the horn with one hand and held the reins in the other. When he reined the horse to a stop, he slid off the saddle and walked to stand next to Cole.

"I've only seen one of these in sketches." He gazed upon the brass weapon with his mouth open in awe. "Unbelievable. Little wonder it is so formidable. I cannot believe we survived. Imagine an army of these."

"The Army is the only one that got them. They must have stolen this one somewhere. Probably more men needing burying wherever it come from."

"Do you know who this man is?" asked Richard, pointing at the blond dead man.

"Nope. Never saw him before. Got to think he was one of Dallas's gang. There's some tracks that show someone else was up here, too. Likely as a spotter for this one to fire the gun." Cole nodded in the direction of the tracks. "Whoever it was, he rode at a gallop to spread the news that they don't have this anymore." Cole went to the palomino. "We need to stay as close as we can."

"Now we need to stay close to them? Before you said it was a bad idea to follow so close."

"And look what it brung. They've already played that card. We ain't got no food. Wherever it is these tracks lead, likely there is something to eat. Now's the time to get as near as we can." He looked to the dead man. "Especially since things didn't go all their way." That said, Cole put a foot in the stirrup, but he stopped when he saw Richard attempt the same.

The sorrel nervously reared and circled from the direction of the jabbing camera legs. Finally, Richard recognized the reason for the horse's temper. He tried to straighten the long wood sticks, but the lopsided load kept sagging at one end or the other.

"Here," Cole said, "let me help." With a firm stride to settle the matter in a hurry, Cole untied the hanks that held the camera in place. "Need to put this in a different spot." With the camera off the horse, he slung it over his shoulder and went to the edge of the ridge, sliding the bound legs in his hand like a spear, and hurled the piece to fly down the slope and crash. The box shattered as it tumbled to a rest at the edge of the embankment.

"One more thing them church folk can bury," he snarled while walking past. "Now, let's ride."

CHAPTER TEN

The pounding of approaching horse hooves drew him to the window. Out of the black of night emerged a rider, reining in his mount from a furious gallop. With the animal at a stop, the rider slid off the saddle and ran toward the front door. Without a clear look at the face, caution required the pistol's hammer to be cocked back and steadied at the door. When it flew open, the dim lantern's light kept the trigger from being pulled.

"Hix? You nearly got your head blown off. Next time, say something before you come barging through that door."

With his hands belatedly raised, the panting rider looked about at the other men in the small one-room shack. "Sorry, Coy. I just needed to get here quick." Catching his breath, he gulped so as to be able to speak. "Tanner's dead."

"What?" He steadied the pistol again at

Hix, as if to threaten the truth. "The hell you say. What are you talking about?"

Hix nodded, not anxious to make any quick moves with a muzzle pointed at his belly. "I saw it myself. Yesterday afternoon. They killed him."

"Who killed him? You better start making sense."

Slowly, Hix slowed his breathing and lowered his arms. "We stayed on the ridge. Set up the Gatling gun, just like you left us. And then we waited. A gang of men came riding into the valley. Looked to be Pinkertons, like you told us." He paused, eyes darting to the dark corner of the shack and then again at Coy Dallas. "So when they were at the spot, Tanner started cranking the gun. But they started riding fast just before."

"What do you mean? They saw you? Didn't you cover the gun?"

Hix nodded. "We did, we did. I don't know who or how, but they started riding for that gully that was at the bottom, remember?"

"Go on!"

A relieved grin crawled over Hix's face. "That gun started cutting them to pieces. Took two right off their horses. The rest of them fired back, but none of their bullets ever came close to us." The grin faded. "Then, all at once, Tanner's chest blew up. Blood pumped out his back, and when he fell, I could see it pumping out the front of his chest."

"How in the hell can that happen? You just said none of their shots could reach you." Dallas jabbed the pistol muzzle against Hix's nose. "Did you kill him? That what you done, ain't it? You killed him thinking there'd be that less to share in a pot."

"No," Hix said, shaking his head. "No. That ain't what happened. Tanner kept firing that gun. Hit the rest of them as they popped up their heads. But a shot came from the other side of the gully while he was firing. One shot hit the Gatling. Surprised us both. The next one took him right in the chest and killed him dead. That's the truth, Coy. That's why I come to tell you."

After a long breath, Dallas eased the hammer to rest. "Must have been a crack shot."

Hix nodded, keeping his eyes on the revolver. "It was. Didn't sound like no Winchester."

"Sharpe's rifle?"

"Don't know," answered Hix. "Never heard one to know. But whatever it was, it did the job. We must have been more than a half-mile away."

Dallas tucked the pistol in his hip holster. "What did you do?"

With a confused face, Hix shrugged. "I got on my horse and rode straight here."

"You left Tanner there? You didn't stop and see if you could have helped him? You didn't shoot back? You just got on your horse and rode straight here?"

"Tanner was dead, Coy. Nothing I could do could help him. I figured if they shot him, wouldn't be no time before they hit me. I didn't know how to load and fire that Gatling."

"They?"

Hix nodded. "Yeah. Two of them, I think. I can't be sure, but counting the ones I saw killed left two that I didn't see killed."

Coy Dallas gritted his teeth and drew the pistol once more. "You ran like a gutless coward and left a set of tracks leading right here. You stupid son of a bitch." He wrenched back the hammer.

"Don't kill him, Coy," yelled Harper. "We need every gun we can get now with Tanner gone." The leader slid his finger into the trigger guard, not used to being ordered. However, as he steadied the barrel at Hix, he finally closed his eyes, rested the hammer once more, and lowered the pistol.

"You're a damn lucky man, Hix. You may

have cost some of these men their lives by riding here. If there's a bullet meant for them, it'll be your job to stop it or take it for them." He moved the revolver into the holster. "Plans have changed. Now, with men directly on our trail, we're going to have to do different than what we want."

"We going to kill the nig?"

Clem's question brought Dallas's attention to the bound half-breed in the corner. "Not yet. We may need him more than before."

The warmth of the day faded away with the sun. A flicker of light peeped through the night's shroud like a friendly wave. Cole kept the palomino steered straight at the light, anxious for the heat of a fire, a plate of food, and plenty of rest from the day's ride. With Richard close behind, he slowed the horse so as not to spook anyone up ahead by the approach of galloping riders. Once they neared, he recognized that the light didn't come from a farm home or a staging station. Three horses were tethered to hitch posts on the side. He took that as a sign that the place was a gathering spot for men seeking to end the day with talk and liquor.

Although he was reluctant at first, the

brisk breeze convinced him he wouldn't get any warmer welcome outside. As Richard finally came alongside, they both stopped their horses and dismounted. Cole drew the Colt revolver and opened the chambergate to count six fresh brass shells.

"Trouble?" asked Richard.

He tucked the Colt in the holster, then pulled the short-barreled Remington and made sure it was loaded. Finally, he put it back in his coat and looked to Richard. "We'll see."

Cole went to the front, glanced back at Richard, then raised the latch and went inside. At first he saw two men sitting at a table in the far corner. A fire-pit hearth sat in the middle of the log building. A man standing behind a chest-high bar counter to the left appeared to be the proprietor. Before he could look to the right, a booming order came from the owner.

"Raised in a barn, mister? Shut the goddamn door. It's cold outside."

Cole nodded his head for Richard to comply. Once the door was shut, they both took a step closer to the fire. He made it a point to unbutton his coat and let the tin star sparkle in the luminance.

"You men wanting a drink?"

It was more of a sales pitch than invitation. Cole first angled a glance at Richard. Whiskey on a cold night was said to take the chill from bones. However, even a snort had the effect of a whole bottle on him. Despite being with four occupants, he knew he was alone and a clear head was needed. He rubbed his hands together and shook his head. "Just came for the fire, friend. Don't mind, do you?"

The owner didn't smile at the refusal, but didn't complain either. The barrel-chested man wiped down the bar. Cole frequently peeked at the rest of the men, darting his eyes around the room, then back to the flame. The two at the corner table shared the bottle that sat in the center. The table appeared clumsily built, with legs of different widths. Two were sanded round, and the others had squared edges.

One of the men wore a broad-brimmed hat, the other left his on the table. They cast eyes at Cole between their whispers. Richard edged closer to the fire, shifting position from right to the left. When his vision was unblocked, Cole noticed a silhouette of a man in the right corner of the room. Knowing he was more easily in view to the unseen stranger, he kept his eyes from the direction, hoping to bring the stranger out into the light by other means.

"Damn cold night." Richard appeared puzzled by Cole's loud tone. "A whore's heart a week before payday couldn't be any colder."

Without a response, but with all eyes pointed at him, he stepped closer to the bar. "Makes a man ask himself why he would be out on a night like this one. Sure wouldn't be a choice he'd make if he didn't have to." All eyes stared at him, but no mouths moved. At least the three he could see.

"So why are you here?" asked an unknown voice from the dark.

With his left hand on the bar, Cole leaned back against the counter with the owner, the two at the table, Richard, and the silhouette in view. His coat pulled around the holster, he could draw the Colt at anybody in the room, but the reporter needed to move.

"There's a gang of convicts on the loose. Led by a fellow named Coy Dallas. These outlaws have killed more than a dozen men. And some women. I'm looking to stop them, and would be beholden to anyone might be able to tell me where they might be or where they may be headed to."

"What makes you think they're here in these parts?"

The question drew his attention to one of

the two at the table. A bit surprised that the conversation had attracted more than one man's interest, he thought it best to walk closer to the table. As he went, he passed the owner and kept moving so as to not have the barrel-chested man at his back. "I have good reason to think they came through here. Might have rode right outside that door."

The one wearing the hat sneered. "Now, why do you think that, Marshal?"

"Twelve hours ago, two of those men tried to kill me." Cole noticed that the one without the hat sat with both hands drooped between his legs and kept his eyes straight. "They killed six Pinkerton agents. I shot one of them outlaws. The other rode fast in this direction. He's on a tall mount, maybe fifteen hands or sixteen. Could favor its right foreleg in its stride."

The one with the hat shook his head. "Ain't seen nothing of the sort come by here."

"Shame," Cole said, keeping an eye to the darker side of the shack. "I was hoping for some help in finding these fellows." Richard stood with a bewildered expression. Cole sensed trouble was soon to come. The reporter needed to be out of the line of fire. He got Richard's attention, then looked at the door, then back to Richard in attempt to silently steer the tinhorn. The reporter appeared even more puzzled. Finally, Cole closed his eyes.

"How 'bout you, son?" Cole asked, patting the shoulder of the one without the hat. "Seen these men we're after?"

The kid shivered as bad as a cat in a pen full of hounds. Slowly, the young face came turned into view and he shook his head. "No, sir. I never seen nothing." The kid trembled more than natural. So much so, it seemed the answer was less the truth and more what the one in the hat wanted said.

"Sure about that?" More rapid nodding provided the answer, but Cole wasn't convinced. "What be your names, boys?"

"Mine's Robert Ferrel," replied the one with the hat. "This is Sammy. Sammy Turner. What's your name, Marshal?"

"Clay Hayes." Cole peeked at Richard. "And over there is Dick the Dandy Johnson. He's from the East. Don't let his look fool you. He talks all the time about Wild Bill Hickok. Just like he knew the man personal. So he knows how to handle his iron."

"That a fact," said Ferrel, eyeing Richard at the door. "Well, you know, Marshal, I know how to handle my iron, too." Having spoken with an arrogant tone, the kid made it plain he held no fear of a badge, or at least wanted it thought.

"Easy, son," Cole said with a forced smile. "We're all friends here enjoying a warm fire together." He saw an empty chair at the end of the bar and pulled it up next to the table. The position provided a better look at the darker corner of the building, the owner behind the counter, and kept his own back against the wall. The only person he didn't have a good eye on was Richard. "Tell me what kind of line you're in."

As Cole sat between the two young men, Robert Ferrel's arrogance faded into one of desperate ignorance. "We're miners." The response lit up Sammy's shaky face. The friend's expression brought back the arrogance. "That's right. We're miners."

Confident it was a lie, Cole glanced at Robert's clean hands and even cleaner youthful face. "Miners?" He glanced at Sammy's nervous grin. "What mine you work?" It took more than a normal moment before the question was answered.

"The Amazon."

From out of the far dark corner, a figure emerged into the light. A man, older than the two seated at the table, wore a brown broad-brimmed hat like a cattleman. A long, dark blue duster covered his front. The fire's glow showed only one side of his whisker-stubbled face. Once he came fully into the light, he stepped around the pit to stand next to Richard.

"You with these boys?" asked Cole, sliding his hand between the chairs. His coat covered his holster, and to raise it to draw the Colt would also raise the suspicion he didn't trust these men, which he didn't. There wasn't an instant answer to his question. "What's your name, friend?"

"Why you asking all these questions?"

The refusal to answer sent a chill through Cole's nerves. When he had come to the shack, none of the three horses tethered to the post seemed to be an animal capable of the stride to leave the tracks. So confident of his judgment, he didn't consider taking the time to check the shoes for the spur. Had he the luxury, he would have chided himself aloud. However, the next move required would take all the concentration he could muster.

The man in the duster stood square in the line of fire, but the Colt would have to come up through the space between the chairs and clear the table just to come to an aim. "Like I said. I'm looking for a man was part of an ambush on me and Pinkerton agents which killed six men." Cole's low tone

199

didn't change the man's stance or manner. "What you know about that?"

The duster opened. The fire's yellow light showed the coat, but the body was in shadow. Cole dug under his own coat, fingers on the leather holster about the time double shotgun barrels emerged from under the duster to gleam in the light.

Once his hand had a grip of the Colt and he was ready to snatch it and stand to fire, the scattergun pointed at Richard.

"You move again and I'll paint this wall with this one's guts."

Cole seized his own right arm, not knowing if the barrels were about to swing his way. He steadied his breath and eased back in the chair. "You the one up on that ridge?"

An instant passed before a grin cracked the shotgun shooter's face. "Still sticking to that story, Marshal?" He bobbed his head to the side. "Get his gun, Sammy."

While both boys found and removed the Colt and the .36, Cole sat confused as to what he had stumbled in on. "Just who are you, then?"

The cock of his own Colt filled his left ear. "We is the ones that took two thousand dollars out of the Amazon payroll office," Robert Ferrel proudly admitted while holding the pistol.

"Shut your mouth."

The shotgun was pressed harder against Richard's chest with one hand, while the shooter wearing the duster pointed at Ferrel. The reporter darted his eyes between the shooter and Cole. Without a weapon, there was nothing that could save him. Cole stared into Richard's eyes, awaiting the loud blast that would tear the Easterner in half. With a gun muzzle poked against his own ear, he blinked and dipped his view to the point of the shotgun's barrels, then lower to where Richard's hand was tucked inside his coat's side pocket. Cole blinked again, and once more looked into Richard's wide, panicked eyes. Those eyes appeared to ask the question of what to do next. Cole nodded.

Fire streamed out of the coat. A loud blast turned the attention of the two at the table. The duster-wearing shooter fell back into the fire pit. Cole shoved his elbow into Ferrel's nose, then snatched the bottle on the table by the neck, striking it against the table edge to shatter it in half. With a sweep of a punch, he stabbed the jagged points into Sammy's throat. The boy's wail pierced the air, loud at first, then fading into a gurgling cough.

Cole wheeled about just as Robert Ferrel

regained balance. He rammed his boot's heel into the kid's chest, slamming Robert against the wall and spilling the Colt to the floor. Now, with his revolver back in hand, he cocked the hammer and pointed it at Robert's chest.

"Don't kill me," shrieked the kid, hands in front of his face. As Cole stood ready to pull the trigger, the stench of burning hair wafted into his nose. He glanced over his right shoulder. The duster was aflame.

"Get that body out of here before the shack burns down!"

Richard hesitated.

"Do it now!"

The command snapped the reporter out of his fright. Richard charged at the dead shooter's body, grabbed the smoldering lapels, and dragged the fiery corpse out the door.

With his attention again on the cowering kid, Cole saw the owner pop his head above the bar. He pointed the Colt at the new target. The barrel-chested man held his hands up high as well.

"Don't shoot me neither, Marshal."

"What's your part in this?"

The owner nodded his head in Robert's direction. "Him and his friends came in here not more than ten minutes before you.

I was about to go home to my missus when they came through and ordered that I serve them. When I refused, they flashed their gunmetal at me. When you rode up, that one with the shotgun said he'd kill me if I said a word and went and sat in the dark."

Satisfied the big man was telling the truth, Cole put his mind back on Robert. "So you're a thief. Robber of mine payroll," he said with spite. "Why did you have to jump us?"

The question appeared to confuse the kid. "You're a damn marshal. We was sure you were after us."

Reminded in an instant that the badge pinned to his chest meant he represented the law to all bandits and outlaws for whatever crimes they had claimed, Cole closed his eyes and let out a deep breath. When he took the moment in thought, it seemed best to use the opportunity he now held to all benefit possible.

He took a step, then bent to clutch Robert Ferrel's collar and lift him from the floor, poking the Colt under his chin. "Where were you headed?"

"Where?" was the dazed reply. "What are you talking about?"

"Where'd did you plan on going?" Cole shook him. "You robbed the payroll. You didn't think nobody would notice? Them miners sure will miss that money in your pockets. So where is the money you stole? Where'd you plan on taking it?"

"I don't know."

The denial tactic infuriated him. "You're going to join your friends," he said, pushing the barrel further against the throat. "You ain't no good to me without the information. I'll give you to the count of three. It's as long as my arm can hold you. One."

Ferrel's right eye angled down in order to see below his chin. "It's the truth, Marshal. Besides, you can't shoot me without a cause. You got me with no gun. You have to take me to jail."

"Too damn far to march you back to jail. Take more than a week. A week more than I got. Just as easy to shoot you here and tell the judge you tried to kill me. Shouldn't be hard to believe. Two."

"I'm telling you I don't know. It was Butler's call where we was going. The whole job was his idea. Sammy and me was to meet him here."

A squeak brought attention to the door. Richard, his face seized with a look of horror, walked back into the cabin. Cole looked back at Ferrel. "And that's Butler out there already burning on his way to Hell?"

Ferrel inched up a nod. "I don't know where he was taking the money. All was said was we'd split it up at Baker's Crossing."

"Where?"

"It's a ghost town north of here," the owner eagerly offered. "Ain't been anybody up there in more than ten years. Once it was thought there was gold there in the streams, but it played out in a few months and after none was found, it was given up. Just a wood bridge is all that's left."

Cole let Robert Ferrel slump to the floor. He faced about and pointed at the shotgun on the floor. "Give it here." Richard followed the order, tossing the weapon with both hands. Cole caught it with one, then handed it to the owner stock first. "How far is this Baker's Crossing?"

"Better than fifty miles from here."

Cole nodded his understanding. "Got any grub?"

"Jerky is all I keep here."

"I'd be obliged for all you can spare."

The owner leaned under the counter for an instant and returned with a canvas sack he placed on the bar. "Take it all, Marshal. It's the least I can pay for saving my skin."

"Appreciate that," said Cole, swiping the sack with one hand, then walked toward the door. He motioned for Richard to leave.

"Hey, Marshal," the owner asked, turning Cole about, "what do I do with him?" Cole looked to Robert Ferrel and shrugged.

"Have him bury his friends. After that, he's yours to deal with as you like." Cole opened the door and pushed the stunned Richard outside. With huddled shoulders, he marched past the smoldering duster-clad body to the palomino and routinely tucked the jerky sack into his saddlebags.

"Dick the Dandy Johnson?"

Cole faced about to the rigid standing reporter. He cocked his head to the side. "I thought it clever at the time. What do you think?"

"I killed a man! I killed a man, and you speak of being clever. How dare you. Have you no reverence?"

Although understanding the remorse and shock of bringing death to another no matter the circumstance, he didn't need to argue the matter. The best approach was loud and firm. "You did what you had to do. He'd killed you just the same and wouldn't be feeling nearly as poorly as you. You done good. Now, let it pass. It's what's done out here. A man has to do what's needed, and you sure did. Got both of us out of there alive with all our pieces still together." He gave Richard's shoulder a light backhanded tap. "Now. Get mounted and let's head north."

"You're going to ride fifty miles to go where there is nobody."

Cole stepped into the stirrup and pulled himself into the saddle. "I've got a hunch. With all this killing, Dallas hasn't got no time to be robbing on his own. It just may be he's depending on a little help from his brotherhood of thieves."

Richard got onto his sorrel. "So we are to ride in the middle of the night based on the story of one of those thieves? A thief that nearly killed us?"

"And most of tomorrow, too. Sometimes those are the best to follow. Especially when they smell a bullet aching to split their head open."

Richard came alongside. "Are you sure you can leave our fate on just that?"

While nudging the palomino, Cole glanced back. "Would you lie if you had a gun pointed at your head?"

CHAPTER ELEVEN

Hands bound behind him, Choate struggled for strength to keep himself in the swaying saddle. No food for nearly two weeks had weakened him worse than he'd ever known. Just to keep his head raised required proud will.

The gang rode two days, each man stopping only long enough to do their nature and catch up with the rest. They ate hard bread in the saddle. The one called Dallas stayed at the front. When he stopped, all stopped. When he moved, all moved.

Sunlight seeped away from the second day as they neared a tall hill. Choate's horse was led by the third rider. Once they reached the top, all stared at the small town below.

"He's down there, boys." Dallas pointed at the middle building in a row that stood taller than all others. "I'll bet he's having his supper right about now."

"When are we going to leave?"

The question turned Dallas's anger-taut face back to the second rider. "Leave? What are you talking about, leaving? We just got here."

"I mean leave the territory. The law's after us. Won't be long before they track us down. We'll all be at the end of a rope if we don't head north instead of stopping."

The notion curled the lips of the leader. Choate watched for iron to be drawn in response, but Dallas's hands stayed on the reins. "You do what I tell you, and there'll be plenty of time to head north with a pack full of silver." He angled his head back at Choate. "Bring him along for the show." He took out his anger on the horse and the rest of the riders followed.

The gang rode down the slope to the edge of town. Darkness allowed the glow of lanterns to guide them through the streets. Upon reaching the tallest building, they dismounted. Choate, without benefit of use of his hands, raised his right leg over the saddle and slid down. The third rider shoved him onto the boardwalk. With the men huddled next to the door, Dallas gave all a last look and drew his piece.

The door had fine glass in the center, with drapes covering the interior light. Dallas turned the knob and threw it open. The men marched in quickly. Two men sat on narrow chairs, both holding newspapers. Their startled faces popped up from behind the print. Dallas aimed at the nearest.

"Where's Carlyle?"

The one at aim shook his frightened, puzzled face. "I don't know any man by the name." Dallas changed the aim to the other and got the same answer.

"I said, where's Carlyle?" he shouted. "Judge Amos J. Carlyle. I got wind he's staying here. Everybody in the territory knows the man. Old, thin as a stick, gray hair all fluffed up to one side. No beard. No mustache."

A fat man came from a hall, dressed in a white shirt and a gold-sparkled vest. He stopped and was as shocked as the others at the sight of the gang all with pistols drawn. "What is the meaning of this? You're in the Parker House Hotel. If you want the saloon, there's five of them just down the street. You can't come in here with guns. There's a city ordinance. A law against the carrying of firearms in town. And you can't bring no blacks indoors. You boys can get into a lot of trouble."

The brash talk forced Dallas to slowly step toward the fat man, gradually pulling back the hammer of his revolver to poke it against the fat man's nose. "I'm looking for the law. Matter of fact, I'm looking for the man that doles it out. Judge Carlyle. Now, tell me where he is."

Shivering as with fever, the fat man shook his head. "I'm — I'm not sure he's here. He may have stepped out. Are you friends of his?"

The question brought a grin to Dallas's face. He looked back at his gang. "Go in every room. Find the son of a bitch and bring him down here."

"That won't be necessary." The voice turned all attention to the stairs. There stood the man Dallas described on the bottom step. "Hello, Coy."

"Howdy, Judge," came the answer with a smile. "Good to see you remember me."

"It's hard to forget a man who kills innocent people to take what doesn't belong to him. You weren't the only one, but you were the worst."

Choate looked to Dallas's pistol, waiting to see it spit fire at the remark. Instead, Dallas calmly put it in the holster and approached the old man.

"You see, Judge, that's how all you folks look at things. You only see them from your own way. Now, to me, them mining companies had what I wanted," he paused to grit his teeth, "what I needed." He relaxed his tone. "The way I look at it, they have all the money they could ever need, and I just wanted a little part. The ones that got in the way had it coming for not seeing it my way." Again, he paused to allow his grin to grow once more. "Now, that's the way I see it."

"What is it you want, Coy?" the judge asked with a booming tone. "If it's me, then let's get to it. It's what I've expected since I heard you busted out. You can leave these people to their peace. I won't fight you."

Dallas's grin grew bigger. "Right neighborly of you, Judge." He reached for his pistol. "I may just shoot you here and be on my way."

"Coy," said the second rider. The loud call turned all heads his way. "There's food here. Beds, too. We ain't ate or slept a night for three weeks."

"What are you talking about, Clem? Just say what you're meaning."

"I'm saying there's no need to leave. At least, not just yet. You kill him now and we're going to have to light out of here."

Again, Dallas first scowled, then lightened his face. "Clem, that's a right smart idea." He returned his face to the judge. "It looks you got a reprieve." He shoved the old man farther into the lobby. "Hix, you go and find out if there's any real law in this town. If so, bring him here. The rest of you search about and find something to eat. Go upstairs and find you a bed. If there's a man in it, yank him out of it. If there's a woman in it, you can keep her in it." He grinned at the judge. "Let's have some fun."

Darkness had fallen before the warmth of the day could be appreciated. Through the pitch of night, Richard followed Cole up and over the endless mounds and hills. Afraid to speak for risk of being left alone, he did his best to blink in any light possible to view his surroundings. The wind brought cold with the speed of a runaway train and sealed the air with its frigid grip. Only feet ahead, he managed to keep sight of the palomino's fair tail.

His hands shook holding the reins, but only in part due to the temperature. Although he attempted to flush it from his mind, he couldn't rid himself of the thought of killing a man. It was an instinctive reaction and he was thankful for the outcome. Still, he'd fired a bullet into a human being. Despite the stiff breeze, the pungent smell of burning flesh and cloth stained his nostrils.

The need to cleanse his soul of guilt was restrained by the fear of another rebuke from Cole. The repulse at the sight of death before his very eyes didn't seem to bother this gruff frontiersman. A confession would only bring about more of his disdain for compassion at the loss of human life.

In order to relieve his conscience, he concentrated more on his dislike for his partner on this journey. At one time, he was fascinated by the likes of him. The mystery of how these men went about their lives fueled his curiosity and that of the thousands who read their adventure stories. Even though he was well aware that most of the stories were obviously written to feature a chivalrous manner, he expected some redeeming qualities. So far, he recognized little if any to be admired. Clay Cole was no knight.

The bitter slap of wind huddled his shoulders. Nothing could be seen in the dark to distract his attention, so he blinked his tearing eyes and focused on that fair tail.

Men laughing and screams of women echoed into the dark room. Choate leaned against the wall. Although weak, he struggled against the rope binding his hands. While the gang enjoyed the warmth of a roof, whiskey, and the women they found, he used the chance to free himself. He didn't have long.

He peered into the dark square room. A wooden stand with an unlit kerosene lamp stood next to the bed. Over his shoulder he saw the rope strung from his hands tied to its iron frame. Even if he had the strength to get to his feet, the noise of dragging the bed across the wood floor would attract too many ears.

Frustration drained his spirit as much as his hunger. When he rested his head against the wall, a sparkle caught his eye. Through the window, a beam of light reflected off the glass lamp chimney shade. The moment of irritation planted a seed in his brain. As silently as possible, he pushed against the wall, one leg extending far enough to slide up so as to extend the other.

Once propped against the wall, he took in breath to steady his shaky arms. He rolled his shoulders to turn his back to the lamp. He edged nearer the stand. His fingers arched out and he closed his eyes to concentrate. Glass shattering could bring back his captors.

Another step and his thumb bumped a firm surface. He took another breath and carefully put his fingers on the lamp, but as he rose, the weight of the bed's iron frame kept him from a full stance. In order to grasp the lamp with both hands, he bent forward and locked his elbows, forcing his arms as far back as possible. Gradually, he wrapped his fingers around the lamp.

Bending further allowed him to lift it from the stand. Scooting his feet to the side, he angled a path to the bed. He took a step back, then another. When the back of his knees hit the edge of the mattress, he fell back holding the lamp against his back. When he collapsed, he felt the glass shatter, his own body muffling the sound.

He gritted in pain as shards sliced into his palms. The warmth of blood trailed over his fingers, but he fumbled with the edges until he recognized a textured edge along his fingertip. He twisted the edge against the rope.

The odor of kerosene seeped into his nose at the same time it stung his open wounds. Pain shot through his spine as the fuel soaked the blanket and his flesh. He pushed the single shard back and forth, sawing into the hemp. His muscles trembled and his fingers became numb. Still, he continued and fought the cramps in his hand.

Voices approached. He peeked down at the light under the closed door. Shadows broke into the steady beam. As the low voices grew louder, he hurried, but his strained fingers didn't respond. Bright light spilled into the room, illuminating his body bent backward over the bed. Figures stood silhouetted in the doorway.

"What are you doing, nig?" asked the familiar voice of Coy Dallas.

Choate lay still, too exhausted to fight or run, uncertain if they had come to kill him.

"What smells in here?" Dallas came to the bed and snatched Choate's shoulder to roll him over on his side. "Look here, Hix. This boy was trying to escape. Cut himself up pretty good doing so at that." He pushed Choate back. "What's the matter, nig? You don't like us?" He glanced behind, then returned his stare into Choate's eyes. "Hix here found the local sheriff. Learned some interesting news. Word has spread that somebody called the Rainmaker is out looking for you."

"Cole?" murmured Choate.

Dallas nodded. "Well, it appears he's on his way. A couple of my men think they heard of this fellow. Bad hombre, so they say. Once they heard his name, they thought he's the one that might have killed Tanner. If he is, then I want to meet him." He leaned closer and spoke through gritted teeth. "I want to meet him real bad." The gritted teeth went to a wide smile. "Which is good news for you. I was going to lynch you right here and be done with you. But now, it seems you're just what I need to make that happen."

"Bait."

"That's right." He grabbed Choate's shoulder and yanked him from the bed to shove him toward the door. "Hix, tell the boys that we're leaving."

"Leaving?" Hix asked as he caught Choate and kept him from falling to the floor. "Hell, Coy, we just got here."

"I don't want to be caught in no place I can't see what's coming for miles. Tell them to sober up and get to their saddles. We're going to fire the town. The Rainmaker wants to find me. He's going to have to come to where I want to be found. And we're going to leave him something to follow."

Cole lit a match. He cradled the flame in cupped hands and leaned closer to the dirt while on one knee. The glow illuminated his face. Within a minute, he shook the flame out. "Ain't no tracks leading here."

Richard dismounted in part to join Cole in the dark and to rest his backside. Once there, he noticed Cole looking at a wood

218

bridge spanning a creek no wider than a hundred feet. "I thought there was a town around here?"

"Likely across the bridge yonder. No light coming from there. It appears that bartender was right. But that no-good kid wasn't." He shook his head.

Richard knelt next to Cole. "He probably didn't know everything, just as he said."

"Maybe."

"I mean, you did put a gun to the man's head. I would be saying anything that came to mind. Anything that you wanted to hear in order to get that gun away from my head."

It took a moment and a concentrated focus to see, but Cole grinned at the remark. "That may be the case, too."

Although the change of expression was a pleasant diversion, the strong wind reminded him of the matter at hand. "So now where do we go?"

"I don't know, Richard" was the terse reply. "You ask that at least ten times a day. Don't expect an answer every time you ask it. Because I don't rightly know."

"I only asked a question." He didn't want to pour more fuel on the fire, but there were legitimate complaints. "We've been riding almost two solid days with no rest. All because you believed that Dallas would be here to get stolen money. Now that we're here and there's no sign of Dallas or his men, I was naturally curious what you planned next." The more he vented, the more complaints came to mind. "I have not eaten nor slept for an appreciable time for almost four days. I, too, am very weary of this continual episode where I am shot at by outlaws and frightened within an inch of my life. I'm exhausted following you over this vast wasteland for days on end."

Cole pointed his finger. "You're the one that wanted to come along. Paid for it with your last dollar. And a damn fool for it. Ain't my fault it wasn't what you thought it would be," he said, then looked over his shoulder.

The assertions were accurate, but the irritating cold kept Richard's mood bitter. "Yes. But I expected some level of expertise." Cole turned about with a quizzed expression, as if not understanding the statement, or so it seemed to Richard in the dim light. "Forget it." He switched his anger to that which really bothered him. "How long will this wind last? It's hasn't stopped for almost four nights. It is still August."

Cole stood and faced into the howling wind. "It's a storm maker. Coming from up north in Canada. It'll reach as far south as Texas by the end of the week." It sounded as if he chuckled, but there was no visible evidence of it. "I remember ten years ago standing about this same place. I was trooping for the Army. We'd attempt to bivouac along these hills. Then a big norther like this one would come through and send them canvas tents a tumbling down the slope." The laugh seemed a bit louder and more giddy. "Many a time I told myself I'd never be back. Now look at me."

Although the voice held a tone of levity, the meaning sounded bittersweet. "But you did return, didn't you?" There was a long pause without response. Richard feared he had brought about the painful memories that had become legend. In an instant, he was reminded he was in the presence of the traitor of the Seventh Cavalry.

Cole went to his horse. "Yeah, I did. Had no choice." When he passed to the other side of the palomino, Richard rose and followed to see. Cole flipped up the stirrup to tighten the cinch. "The Army needed scouts, and I was one that knew the lay of the land."

The simple remark wasn't satisfying. "You scouted for Custer, didn't you?"

Despite the pitch black of night, Cole's

face seemed as clear as if it were in the brightness of day. A scowl lined his lips. "What do you want to ask me? I know you've been champing at the bit to ask." He neared, and the stench of his breath blew into Richard's face. "You want me to tell you what happened? You want to know what it was like in that valley? Women and kids screaming and crying? Gunshots pounding the ears? Soldiers and Lakota trading fire? Heads blown apart like melons? Men with their bellies ripped open, their guts spilling out into the dirt? Is that what you want me to tell you? 'Cause if it is, I'm ain't a-going to. It ain't something you or them that reads your books has got to know." He took down the stirrup off the saddle seat.

Richard stood more frozen by the tirade than by the wind. As he watched Cole climb into the saddle, he felt paralyzed — not only unable to move, but uncertain if he should continue to follow. Had he just momentarily angered this man, one accustomed to killing, or had he given reason to be shot? His own right hand slipped into the coat pocket with the bullet hole and clutched the pistol.

"You coming?"

Richard wasn't sure of the answer but couldn't speak a word of his indecision.

"Well, come on. Let's move."

The tone sounded minutely more friendly, yet it could have been a ruse to have him turn his back. He stayed put, hoping the cover of darkness would hide his shivering.

"Like you said, it's clear they ain't here. We've got to find some place where we can find food. That means we ride."

With the wind whipping into his face, the minor change in Cole's voice made Richard consider mounting the sorrel. However, he couldn't muster the strength to take the first step.

"Hurry, will you. We'll have to cover a heap of ground. And it ain't like someone's going to give us a map to follow."

Richard dipped his head, rationalizing the truth of circumstance. As he stood, the silhouette of the palomino's hooves came into view. Then more definition of the surrounding grass. The odd sensation made him wonder if dawn had broken. He lifted his view, and there was Cole in the saddle with his head turned to the west. Richard, too, looked in that direction.

The yellow glow emerged from over the crest of a far hill, illuminating the sky above like a great haze. "What is it?"

As before, the answer didn't come at once. More than a noticeable moment passed before Cole's voice muttered a single word in a foreboding tone.

"Fire."

CHAPTER TWELVE

The morning's light faded the blaze's luminance, but gray smoke spiraling in the calmer breeze kept them on course. As they rode on the plain, shapes emerged from the distance with each loping stride of the horses. Cole knew what to expect.

Surrounded by hills to the north, the remains of a small town became discernible as they approached. He slowed the palomino to a walk as he came into the main street. The horse became skittish as he went farther into the town. Charred wooden buildings smoldered, each butted against the other. There was little wonder that if one burned, they all burned. While he eyed the ruins, he coughed from the heated air and smoke, his eyes teared, and the inside of his nostrils felt singed. He raised the red bandanna over his nose, then peeked behind for Richard to do the same.

The townsfolk were scattered about in the

street. Some still ran with buckets, trying to drown the last small flames and embers. When he and Richard rode in, all eyes they passed stared in fear. Through the smoke, he saw a crowd huddled at the end of the street. Needing information, he steered toward them.

When he stopped the palomino, an elderly man wearing a scorched apron rose from his knees and held up his hands. "We haven't got anything. Can't you see?"

To keep down panic, Cole pulled down the bandanna and opened his coat to show the badge. "Federal marshal. What happened here?"

The one with the apron dropped his face into his hands and began bawling like a newborn. Two other men and a woman remained on their knees surrounding what looked to be a body. The woman, strands of brown hair drooped in front of her face, angled her head at him. "They burned the town. They hung Judge Carlyle."

Alarmed, Cole dismounted and went to the body on the ground they were around. The frail fellow lay limp, his face smeared with soot, a purple red bruise encircling his throat. "How long ago did this happen?"

"Nearly three hours ago," said the woman, fighting the thick smoke and the awful memory. "A band of outlaws took over the hotel, shot up the place, then set fire to it. The wind spread it to every place in town. Nobody had a chance. Some folks didn't get out before the flames lit their clothes afire."

"Coy Dallas done this?"

"We never learned their names. But every one in town suspects it was him."

"This man was the judge at the trial?"

She nodded, sniveling her nose clear, then looked deeply at Cole and spoke in a calm voice. "Are you the one called the Rainmaker?"

Surprised by the question, he nodded. "Why you ask that?"

She inhaled a breath with noticeable effort, perhaps to choke back tears. "People heard the sheriff tell one of the band that. Shortly after the gang learned the Rainmaker was after them, they set the fires."

He closed his eyes, in part from the shame that again his legendary reputation had caused so much harm. He opened his eyes to see tears welling in hers. "I'm sorry for your loss." He put his hand on her arm, but she slowly recoiled from his attempt to comfort. He pushed his hat back from his face and kept his eyes aimed at the dirt. "Where is this sheriff you spoke of?"

The question sparked more sobbing from her. Choked from crying, she collapsed to the dirt, her face buried in the chest of the dead man. The fellow nearest him pointed at the smoldering hotel. Gradually, Cole looked over his shoulder at the blackened structure. The gesture made apparent that no one in authority was around to help him.

He peeked up at the solemn-faced Richard. If they left now, he'd come a far piece just to view more of the devil's work dealt by Dallas. Despite the loss of life, more intrusions into these folks' grief needed to be made. Cole had to have more answers.

"Did you see a black man with them when they left?"

The inquiry brought the woman from her tears enough to raise her head and point her flushed face to him. "What?"

"A black man. Maybe wearing what looked like Indian buck clothes. Probably looking to be their prisoner."

"A black man?" the nearest fellow asked. "Why would you want to know about a black man? Especially if he was their prisoner. Was he one of their band?"

"No, he wasn't," Cole snapped. "He's a friend of mine."

"A friend? A black man? Is he a lawman, too?"

"No." There was no simple answer to provide these people who had lost so much. "All I want to know is if he was with them." He turned his view from one to the other, looking for some sign they understood, but only confusion was etched in their faces — perhaps due to their frame of mind in the midst of the tragedy that befell them, or just his concern for a darkie when so many of white skin had been killed.

"Yeah," said the third fellow, "I saw him. He was led around by a rope around his neck, and his hands were tied behind his back."

While the other two turned their curious faces to the man with the knowledge, Cole blurted another question before intimidation led to silence. "Then he's alive. He wounded?"

The third fellow scratched his chin. "I didn't get a good look at him. What with the fire and all spreading so fast. But," he said, shaking a finger, "he did appear like he was drunk. You know, stumbling when he stepped. Of course, the one leading him didn't appear to want to help him none. He just yanked on the rope to keep in step."

Cole glanced at Richard, then back at all three of them. "Did these men take anything? I mean, take any supplies with them before they left?"

The fellow that was near shook his head. "Just some liquor. Which they didn't pay for, neither, so I heard. I don't recall seeing them in the store before it burned down. Now, the hotel, it would have had food, if that's what you're asking."

Cole nodded. "It is." He stood. "In all this talk they let spread about me, I don't suppose they mentioned where they were headed."

"No," said the near one. "But the last I saw them, they turned for the border."

"Border?" Richard asked.

"Canada." He stood and pointed at the far hills. "It's but another twenty miles."

The news was sketchy at best, but it was all he had to follow. A quick scan of the town showed there wasn't anyplace left untouched by flame in which to rest or resupply. "Anywhere's we can get some food between here and there?"

"My place is a couple miles from here," said the third one. "I'd be glad to give you what I can spare."

"I'd be beholden to you. I'd see you are paid when I put in for expenses."

He waved his palm. "No need. It would be my honor to feed the law in pursuit of criminals." He pointed to a horse, and Cole,

230

lost for suitable words in parting, just nodded to the other two still kneeling around the judge's body. He was about to mount when the woman's voice stopped the boot from sticking into the stirrup.

"I want you to kill them, Marshal."

Surprised by the stern tone, Cole put both boots on the ground and peered into her bloodshot eyes.

"It's all I ask."

Afternoon settled in. Cordial but respectful good-byes had been said along with the due appreciation for a dinner of potato soup and the gift of a small sack of apples. The host, introducing himself by the name of Watson, again pointed the direction believed taken by the Dallas gang.

Cole, with Richard behind, kept the pace steady to reach the border by nightfall. He pondered the details given during the meal. By Watson's count, there were five men in the gang, including Dallas. How well they were armed couldn't be determined in the panic of their escape. The reason for the direction they chose was also left to reckoning, although the benefits appeared easy to spot.

Without proper cause, those patrolling the border wouldn't have need or want to track down foreigners wanted in another country. By Cole's own knowledge, Canada had less folks living in it than there were in Montana, and thus fewer eyes to spot suspicious persons.

The more advantages piled up in his mind, the less chance he gave for finding them or, for that matter, Choate. He let his eyes drift to the side and rear. Richard appeared asleep in the saddle. It was a welcome sight, as long as he didn't fall from the saddle and force Cole to stop. The more the reporter slept, the less nosy questions were asked.

Dark settled in. Without visible clues to follow, Cole camped on as flat and comfortable ground as he could see at dusk. Richard needed no encouragement to stop. Once off the sorrel, he made good use of that flat ground to continue his nap. A bit irritated at having to make camp alone, Cole took the duty as payment for a peaceful night.

The next day began as those before had. The night had been calm, which led to a cloudless, mild summer day. They continued the journey north, up long sloping green hills, many adjacent to rocky buttes carved from centuries of wind and rain. Richard, although awake, still appeared weary from the weeks in the saddle. The apples gave him something to distract him, but by the end of the day their hunger had emptied out the sack save one.

The sunlight faded, but not the rolling plain ahead. A clutch of tall cedars attracted Cole's eye and he made camp under their broad limbs. A small stream, which explained the presence of the trees, threaded through the surrounding grass. He filled their canteens while Richard reconnoitered for firewood. Without coffee or a pot, the night's meal would be hot water and what was left of the jerky.

He was surprised by the reporter's cache of wood, and they soon had it ablaze. Cole found a rock the size of his palm and placed it near the edge of the fire. The action brought about the return of Richard's curiosity.

"What are you doing?"

"Boiling water." Cole hoped the simple answer would satisfy, but it took a glare to keep further questions from being asked. Next, Cole sought and found a bare spot in the brush. He took his knife and began to dig.

"Do you have any idea where we are?"

He pecked away at the dirt before considering the question. "Well, you know we've come further than twenty miles. But exactly where, I can't tell you." He kept stabbing the ground to enlarge the hole.

"Do you think we'll ever catch them?"

Though it was asked with an honest manner, Cole let the question hang in the air and kept digging, not wanting doubt to take over his head. Once he had completed the circle in the ground to his satisfaction, he went to his saddle. "Yeah, I think we'll catch up with some of them." He untied his bedroll and unfurled it. "A lot depends on them. If they keep their band together, then they'll be harder to catch." He took his slicker from the roll and went back to the hole. "But that's easier said than done."

"What do you mean by that?"

"They're all criminals. They ain't of the same mind." He laid the slicker over the hole, pushing and flattening that which covered the hole to form a bowl. "They ain't got the same purpose."

"I don't understand. And exactly what is it that you're doing over there?"

"What I mean is, they all can't be in this for one cause." He returned to a spot near the fire and picked up the canteens. "The only one that got's a real stake in this is Dallas. He's the leader. Them others had to be promised something big in order to help him." He went back to the hole and opened the canteens, pouring water to fill the depression in the slicker.

"And what do you think that is?"

"The only thing that gets theirs or anyone else's notice. Money. And a heap of it." He went back to the fire and sat on the ground.

"Now what are you doing?"

Cole looked to the rock, then shrugged. "Waiting."

"On what?"

"Well, the way I reckon it, soon or later them boys are going to get tired of following Dallas around with nothing to show for it. That type normally gets bored with a life on the run. They can't have any more food than we got, and they have more mouths to feed. Tempers will start to flare. Soon after, there's going to come a nut-cutting. One or more is going to have had enough, and they'll either leave the bunch or try to take over. But that's going to come with a price."

"They'll have to kill Dallas."

Cole nodded with a wink. "He can't let one leave and get caught by the law, nor can he split up due to the same reason. If he has means to pay them, likely as not they'd have split up already."

Richard raised his brow. "So it makes sense that he's told them they will get paid at some time later."

"Something to that effect. The matter is how long they'll keep believing that. From what I could tell, they left town without gathering any money. Gold or silver coins." He shook his head. "Paper money don't spend in Canada." He took the knife and a long stick, placing the blade under the rock near the fire.

"So why would they come here?"

With the stick atop the rock as a balance, he lifted it with the caution he'd use handling a viper, took two steps, and dropped it into the small pool. Instantly, the water boiled with a sizzle. "Bring your cup."

Richard rose from the ground with cup in hand. He dipped it into the water while Cole retrieved his and did the same. Once both returned to the fire, Cole pulled the sack of jerky from his saddlebag, drew a single strip, and tossed the sack to Richard. He dipped the strip into the cup. "Swirl it around in there. It'll give it some taste, and it tenders the beef."

Richard followed the instruction, slurped the water, and bit off a chunk of the jerky. After a few chews, he grinned. "This isn't so bad. Actually, it's quite good." Cole tore off a chunk with his teeth and chewed on the still-solid meat, rotating it from one side of his mouth to the other.

"You still didn't answer my question."

"What question was that?"

Richard frowned. "Why would he come this far north? Why would he come to Canada?"

Cole shook his head. "I ain't sure." He slurped the hot water, which now held a taste of salty broth. However, it was something warm on a cool night.

With slumped shoulders, he stopped chewing. "All that, and you don't know why they've come here?"

Cole took another bite. It was a nagging question he'd asked himself for the two days since they'd left the town. "I never said it made sense. Except for the notion of escaping the law, it don't." Slurping more water, another idea came to mind. "Want to split the last apple?"

"Why not," the reporter replied with a shrug. Despite the polite acceptance, the offer didn't seem to interest Richard.

Cole reached over his saddle and snatched the apple from the sack. Knife in hand, he slid the blade under his arm to loosen the dirt, then held the blade over the fire. "You know, there are still ten people on that jury that at last count were still alive. I don't think Dallas plumb forgot about them." Apple in one hand, knife in the other, he sliced the fruit in two.

"So back to the enigma of why he came here. If he even is here," Richard said, taking his half and immediately biting into it.

"No," Cole said with a nod. "He's here. That I know. I can feel it." He stared at the apple, but his concentration lay beyond. "My fear is that whenever they break — and they will — they'll decide they can't keep toting Choate." He looked to Richard, whose jaw stopped munching the apple. "And they'll kill him."

Several seconds passed before Richard resumed chewing, finally enough to swallow. "Well," he spoke softly. "Let's hope not. For his sake."

Cole raised his tin. "I'll drink to that." With that, both emptied their cups.

Embers and sparks ascending from the flames lured Cole's eyes upward. Moving light drew attention to the night sky. Directly above, orange and red colors spread and shimmered like a ghostly curtain blowing in the wind. "I'll be damned. You ever seen that?"

Richard gradually raised his head to view the spectacle of dancing light against the stars. "No," he answered with awe. "Have you?"

"One time before. Many years back, when

I was in Montana. But I never seen them this far north."

Always in constant motion, the orange lights faded and shrunk into a bright red ball.

"I have read about them, though. Nobody is sure why they occur. How fantastic."

"Yeah. Once seen a wolverine snarl a grizzly off the same path they both came across. But nothing the same as this." The longer Cole gazed, the more memories flooded his head of the last time he'd seen the lights. He was a trooper back then, and life was a simpler line to follow. Officers gave orders meant to be obeyed, even if doing so meant getting shot or killed. Although not desirable at the time, soldiering left little questions as to what to do next. Now, fifteen years later, he longed for the mundane routine. Had he not chosen to leave the Army, there would be no Little Bighorn in his past. No continual chase to escape that past. No wandering the West in solitude. No loneliness. Maybe with that, the constant uncertainty swirling about in his head would leave him in peace.

More pleasant pursuits filtered into his mind. "What do you know about a place called Australia?"

Richard gradually eased his enamored

face away from the light spectacle in the sky to look at Cole. It took a moment before a sheepish grin crept over his face. "You're asking about that singer back in Copper Springs, aren't you?"

"Just answer the question."

"Well, nothing really. It's far away, I know that. Below the equator a great distance."

Cole swallowed, encouraged by the familiar word. "Yeah, she said that, too. Takes months on a ship to get there." He paused in thought, trying to remember if he'd really heard that or he'd just dreamt it. "Anyway," he said, pausing again and recalling what Stillman had said about the red-haired singer going to Butte to sing, "she ain't there now." More details rushed to mind. He'd been on this trail for near a month. Little doubt she'd moved on to another town. "Where do you suspect these singers go to? Just the towns with men and money that want to see pretty women?"

Richard shrugged, still enjoying the last of the jerky in the steaming water. "I don't know. I suppose. But I happened to see a man named Eddie Foy in Omaha while on the way here. It was quite an amusing show. Maybe they go anywhere that wants good entertainment."

"Omaha?" Cole shook his head, hoping to

rid himself of the doubt. "No, she didn't go that far east. She's going back to San Francisco. Then she's back to this Australia. To see her folks."

Richard raised an eyebrow. "And just how do you know that?"

At once, the certainty of the knowledge vanished. Was it just the wish in his head that planted all he thought he knew? Or had he really shared a bed with the red-haired beauty. He shook his head. "Don't know."

While Richard resumed his fascination with the colored lights in the night sky, Cole pondered what he knew for sure and what he hoped might be. There was more than the desire of the company of a pretty gal needed to turn his life in a better direction. Tired and frustrated, he lay on his bedroll. "Get some shut-eye. Another long day tomorrow."

CHAPTER THIRTEEN

The narrow valley was silent in the morning sunlight. The night's chill wind passed, leaving enough time for the air to soak in some heat. Cole rode with a watchful eye on both modest-sized hills that stood no more than a mile from either side. Richard trailed only ten feet behind, and for the first time in three days appeared more alert. Cole would need him ready the nearer they came to trouble.

While glancing left, he turned back to the right and saw a single rider stopped atop the hill. He reined in. His hand dropped to the butt of the Colt. Richard stopped his horse.

"What is it? What's wrong?"

With his hands still on the reins and pistol, Cole kept his eyes on the motionless rider. "On the hill. To the right. Don't make a move, just look."

A moment passed. "Who do you think

that is?"

More than a minute went by, and Cole pondered while staring at the solitary figure. Even the most foolish of the gang would have seen he'd been spotted. The natural reaction would be to turn tail and alert the rest of the bunch, but this one stood his ground. After at least a full minute elapsed, the rider slowly descended the steep incline toward them. "I guess we're going to find out," said Cole with mild surprise.

The rider's horse carefully stepped down the sharp angles to level ground. As it approached, Cole focused on the outline of the rider. The hat brim was unusually straight and the coat fit tighter around the body than a normal duster. Within a hundred yards, the color red reflected back, and in the next few seconds the rider's identity and purpose were revealed. The rider was adorned in a brass-buttoned tunic, and it was obvious he was no outlaw.

"I think he's a mountie," Richard said with a hint of delight. Despite the increased evidence supporting the statement, Cole didn't release his grip of the revolver.

"Good morning, gentlemen" was the cheery greeting. "Welcome to Alberta. Sergeant Colin Hastings, Northwest

Mounted Police, at your service."

"It's a pleasure to meet you, sir," Richard eagerly replied. "My name is Richard Johnson. I'm a reporter for *Harper's Weekly* of New York City."

The mountie nodded. "Mr. Johnson." His attention turned to Cole.

"Clay Hayes," Cole said, releasing his grip of the pistol and opening his coat. He felt Richard's eyes on his back. "Federal marshal pursuing criminals."

"Surely you must know, Marshal Hayes, that you are more than ten miles from the border with the U.S. You have no jurisdiction here."

The law officer's snippy tone pricked against Cole's mood. "Sergeant, with due respect to your country, the men we're after don't care nothing about who owns the ground they commit their crimes on. They're killers and robbers. Burned a whole town down, killed a judge doing it, not more than fifty miles from here."

"Yes," Hastings replied with a snide smile. "But this is Canadian soil. If these men have done what you say they have, then it will be the duty of the NWMP to find them and deport them back to the U.S. Just who are these men?"

"The only name I know is the leader. A

convict named Coy Dallas."

"Coy Dallas?" The mountie's tone changed from mild curiosity to one of awe mixed with a pinch of fear. "The train robber?"

"The same," Cole replied. "Heard of him, have you?"

It took a few moments before the mountie nodded. "Well, that changes things slightly." He looked first to Cole, then to Richard. "Just the two of you is all that is after him, eh?"

Cole glanced behind and saw Richard dipping his eyes, but he saw no need to apologize. "That's right. There were six Pinkerton agents that were on his trail, too, but they was killed in a gun battle with a Gatling."

"A Gatling gun?"

"Yup. Weren't much of a fight with pistols."

"But," Richard chimed proudly, "the marshal here killed the one firing it."

The mountie eyed Cole. "Is that true, Marshal Hayes?" Cole nodded. The mountie looked down at the Mouton rifle in the scabbard. "With that?"

"Yeah." Cole drew the weapon. "It's a handy device to have at hand."

"It appears an odd design. I've not seen

one like that before. How does it work?"

Initially, Cole was ready to answer the Canadian's question. However, once he thought of the next questions to come — who made the weapon, and how did he get it — he changed his mind. Such questions would lead to just who he was, a subject he didn't want to broach. "Sergeant," said Cole, shoving the rifle back into the scabbard. "We don't have the time to go through all that. We'll leave it that it works good when you need it to." He stared the mountie in the eye. "Now, we're going to need all the help we can get. I don't suppose you got any others like you nearby that can give us a hand in tracking these criminals."

The suggestion made the sergeant pause. "My post is roughly two days' ride east. However, most of the troop are on patrol further to the east and south in search of whiskey runners. It would take at least a week to assemble them into any type of force."

"That's a week we ain't got. But maybe you do. If you was to ride and round up them fellows, it would sure help us out. We'll stay on their trail. As far as I can tell, they're headed straight north."

"Are you sure about that, Marshal Hayes?"

With a shake of the head, he replied, "No. Ain't real sure about nothing."

Hastings pointed to the north. "In the next five miles, you will come to some rough terrain. A range of mountains, a thousand to twenty-five hundred feet high. The farther north you go, the higher the peaks as you get deeper into the Rocky Mountains."

Cole looked in that direction. Suddenly, the pieces all fit. "That's why he's here," he muttered.

"What?" Richard asked.

"That's why he's here." He continued the stare until he was sure he was right, then peered over his shoulder at the reporter. "He's drawing us in. He wants us to follow him up into them hills. Likely knows them like the back of his hand. No telling how many canyons, caves, hidden corners to set up a rifle to pick us off like geese flying by." He inhaled a long breath and huffed it out, pondering what was lying ahead of him. "Sergeant, you'll be doing us a favor if you ride as fast as you can and get the rest of your troop." A pause brought his eyes back to the north. "We're going to head into them hills. Maybe draw some fire, have him give away his position." He dipped his eyes to the ground. "Try not to get shot."

Hastings leaned forward in his saddle,

wearing a cocky smile. "Marshal Hayes, I have what I think is a better plan. You see, I, too, know these hills like the back of my hand. I believe I can be of far better service to your cause as a guide than riding for two days back and fro, eh."

Although it took more than a single moment, Cole finally nodded, welcoming the help. "I reckon that is a better plan, Sergeant Hastings. I'm obliged for your offer."

The mountie shrugged. "After all, this is my country. It is my responsibility for the safety of our citizens."

Cole nodded. "I reckon you're right." He looked again to the north. "We should try to make the base of them hills with still some light in the day. I'm sure they'll have sentries posted. We'll need to see them in the light. Give us some time to find enough scrub. If there's a heap, so much the better." The mountie said nothing, but cocked his head to the side as a gesture of confusion. Cole continued. "We're going to send Dallas a message to come join us. Send him something he's used to seeing."

Hands behind him and lying on his right shoulder, Choate couldn't help but watch his captor squatting by the fire, gulping coffee and slurping hot bacon. Between bites,

Dallas cast a confident eye back to see the half-breed watching.

"Now, nig. I know you're hungry. So why don't you just tell me who this Rainmaker is." He swept a pointed finger around. "Now, the boys here, they think they might have heard of him. They heard stories out of down south of here. About a man with the same moniker who murdered a rancher and all his hands. Raped the man's woman while the rancher's son watched, then shot them both and burned the bodies. Hell, he may have even cooked them for supper. Ate their flesh? This same man killed all the rancher's hands. Shot them dead, all of them, and didn't even get scratched doing it." He paused only long enough to nibble at another piece of bacon, then mumbled while he chewed. "Now me, I don't believe all of that. But I can't figure why such a man would be looking for you. Why you suppose that is? Don't make no sense."

Choate held his tongue. His arm was numb from his own weight, and without food for so long, he hadn't the strength to right himself. The aroma sickened him. The few bites he would earn by telling what he knew wouldn't keep his stomach from gnawing away at itself.

Dallas cracked a grin and shook his head

in the same manner most men did when they heard a funny joke. "You're too damn stubborn, ain't you. Yes, too damn stubborn for your own good." He held up a single bacon strip from the pan with his fingertips. "I'm trying to do what's right. I don't mind sharing. But, nig, you have to share, too. Be neighborly." He propped his head under the strip, lapping at the grease on the end. "Sure is tasty."

Choate kept a stern jowl, careful to match eyes with the leader. The tactic ended the amusement etched on Dallas's face.

"Pride? Is that it?"

"Why don't we just shoot him, Coy?" The voice came from behind Choate and out of his view. Dallas's eyes angled up for an instant.

"No. We ain't going to shoot him. He's just like one of the family now. Like a . . . a . . . dog. Yeah," he said with another grin that lasted only seconds. "He's a dog. My dog." Again, the leader's eyes shot up at the gang member behind Choate. "You see, he keeps denying what he is. He's a no-account bounty hunter. Ain't no law going to come look for him. Besides, he's a nigger. He says he's no nigger, but he looks like one, smells like one. He may be part nigger, which means he's all nigger as far I know. The other part of him looks to be injun. And the law's trying to kill them off as fast they can. So this boy don't realize that he's just a dog." Dallas's eyes peered into Choate's. "My dog." He wiggled the bacon strip. "All I'm asking from my dog is to be loyal. I want him to speak. Tell me about the Rainmaker."

Choate glared at the bristled face of the leader. The words burned inside him. Since he had first understood the white man's language he'd heard the same speech. No words hurt him more. He inhaled as deeply as possible, wanting to scream back, but that would bring more words. More hate. More burn to his gut. If Dallas wanted a dog to speak, then Choate would answer. He let loose of the air in his lungs in a loud wolf howl.

At first, Dallas laughed, and there were other voices laughing. Dallas pointed. "You see, he is a dog."

Choate inhaled again, and again, howling despite the pain in his chest. He howled louder. Louder and longer.

The laughter faded away, but Choate continued. The amusement disappeared from their faces. Dallas scanned the canyon walls to the left and right as the echo carried up and out of the rocks. The leader stood and kicked Choate in the gut. The blow took all the wind inside and the howl with it.

"You think I'm stupid. You think you have friends out there? Friends that will come and help you?"

He kicked again. The toe of the boot jabbed deep into Choate's ribs. Coughing took more air, until there was no more. One moment, then two went by before breath wheezed back into his lungs.

"Here I was trying to be kind. And you betray my kindness with some sort of trick." He knelt atop Choate's chest, restricting any chance for a full gulp of air. "Tell me who he is, nig."

Despite the man's weight pressing down on his chest, Choate sucked in enough air to respond. "He is the wind. The rocks. The clouds, the dust. He sees you now."

Dallas slapped him. "Don't give me none of that injun hooey." He slapped again, snapping Choate's jaw to the side. "And I don't want no sass, neither." He leaned closer and spoke through his gritted teeth. "I want to know: What are you to him? Why is he looking for a nigger? A nigger bounty hunter?" He clutched Choate's hair like reins, steering the face to meet his own. "Tell me, nig. Why does he want you?"

The fire inside him erupted. "He is my brother. We are of the same ground."

Dallas eased his grip only slightly. "What?" he murmured, then laughed as he had once before. "Brother? That man out there is a nigger, too." The laughing stopped, replaced by a shake of the head in doubt. "I ain't believing that. I heard he is white. He's no nig, or even half." Dallas released his grip and stood. "Lying will get you killed, boy." He turned his back and went back to squat next to the fire.

Choate closed his eyes and took slow, deep breaths to relieve the pain. Dizziness stirred his mind. He had said more than he wanted, his heart stoked by the fire of hate inside him. Now the leader heard him speak. What was said was the truth, but it did not matter to this killer white man. Yet when he opened his eyes he saw Dallas sucking on the bacon, like one who claimed a prize. The pain in his chest was small compared to that which ached his heart.

Regret filled Choate's soul. He'd lost what he promised to keep. The leader had his thoughts now. And more would be wanted. A cough tore at his bones. Without food, his mind would grow weaker, and more might come from his mouth. He had to hold on to what was his and not let this white man take it.

"Coy," came from behind. "How long we going to stay here?"

Dallas continued to chew, casting only a momentary glance at the one asking the question. "Just as long as I say."

"Yeah, but with us boxed in this canyon here . . ." The voice paused. "Well, it just makes us an easier target for someone to commence shooting at us." Another glare from the leader made the voice sound like a child's. "I thought we were going to some Canadian town. Calgary, ain't that what you called it? Plenty of food and women? Miner money just for the taking? And no law like in Montana? I thought that's what you promised." Dallas resumed chomping on the bacon, ignoring the questions. The voice now sounded more urgent. "Damn, Coy. We ain't any better off than this darkie. We've been running for near a month now. Sleeping on the ground, eating next to nothing. We ain't seen no money. The law is after us." The more he spoke, the louder his voice became. "I joined up for the pay, not to be riding around killing folks. I ain't no killer. That was your doing. The Rainmaker could be on our trail."

Dallas stood and put his hand on the butt

of his revolver. "Quit your whining. You sound like a woman. I say what goes on in this outfit." Dallas stopped only long enough to clench his jaw, then looked at Choate. "You see what your talk has caused. You get them shaking with talk of this 'Rainmaker.' " He pulled the revolver from the holster. "I'm going to end this talk right now." He cocked the pistol and pointed the muzzle.

Choate closed his eyes. The time had come. He would join his ancestors. This long struggle would end. His spirit would be at peace where all cherished would be one.

"Coy!"

The voice's shout was followed by silence. Without pain, Choate thought he had passed, certain he would feel no more, hear no more. However, the light crackle of the fire was still in his ears. Slowly, he opened his eyes.

Dallas stood and faced about now. Looking at the man, Choate's eyes wandered higher. In the sky, black smoke drifted from the east.

"How far away, do you think?" asked the voice.

After several nods, Dallas, still with pistol in hand, twisted about once more. "At the mouth of the canyon is my guess." He grinned slightly. "He is one smart fellow." Dallas again looked at Choate. "Well, we'll see if he's really your brother."

CHAPTER FOURTEEN

Cole braced his back against the cragged rocks while eyeing the canyon walls below. Rifle in both hands, he glanced behind at Richard. "Can you shoot that pistol?"

The reporter peeked down at the .45 in his grip. "Of course. I've killed a man. Don't you remember?"

"Yeah, well, this won't be just a matter of pulling the trigger. You'll have to aim and hit a target, one that's moving at a distance. Fifty or a hundred feet."

Richard nodded. "I'll hide behind those rocks on the ground," he said, about to move to the position. Cole stopped him by clutching his arm.

"Keep your head down. If those tracks are right, and if that mountie is right about this being a horseshoe canyon, they're going to come out shooting." Cole glanced at the tower of black smoke rising from the bonfire of brush he'd set at the mouth of the canyon. "He knows we're here."

As Richard rose to a crouch, his head turned so he could view the canyon floor, then he dove back beside Cole. "I think you misjudged their interest in the smoke. They're already here."

Cole peeked for himself. A single rider in a black vest and checkered shirt with rifle drawn kept his animal at a slow walk while cautiously searching above. He looked through the gap snaking between the rock walls and saw no further threats. "This one's out as point to draw fire." He next looked to the blaze at the mouth of the canyon. "If that one gets that far, he'll spot us." Cole put the rifle stock to his shoulder.

"You're going to shoot him?" asked Richard with concern. "Kill him, without warning?"

"We only got so much ammunition," he said, glaring over his shoulder. "None to spare as warning shots." He resumed sighting the barrel in line with the rider's chest.

"And if that man is alone and has nothing to do with Dallas?"

The suggestion gnawed into Cole's attention. His gut told him to pull the trigger, to lessen the guns against him. However, doubt seized his finger. In times past, he'd taken the chance a lone gunman stood as a menace and ended the threat before it came to bear. Now the badge pinned to his chest tugged at his conscience. It didn't make sense that a piece of metal should make a difference. Again he sighted his target, closing his left eye for a clear focus. The powerful cartridge would cut through the man's heart, sending most of it out the back. As the rider neared and the range closed, the likelihood of survival would be solely left to the divine. He paused, opening his left eye. He was not divine. Nor had he taken a life unless needed to stop a direct threat to his own, or under orders he'd been taught not to question. With a deep breath and a nagging conscience he'd likely regret, he raised the barrel high and pulled the trigger.

The shot echoed. The rider instantly reined his horse to a stop.

"Federal marshal! Put your hands in the air."

A second after the order bounced off the rocks, the rider kicked the horse to a gallop toward the end of the canyon.

"Thought so," said Cole, pumping the action of the rifle and aiming at the fleeing rider.

A ricochet sprayed bits of stone about and filled the air around him with dust. Cole glimpsed the shooter below, crouching behind a grounded boulder. Another shot brought more debris and dust.

Cole rolled onto his back, only able to cast a single eye down, watching the rider steer through the winding course toward the end.

"Should we warn Hastings?" asked Richard.

"How? If he didn't hear the shots, there's nothing we can do to get him word." Another shot nicked the escarpment. Cole scooted farther from their line of fire.

"Then what should I do?"

"Keep your head down." He rolled back to his original position and fired at the boulder, pumped the action, and fired once more. "And hush." He pumped another shell into the chamber and waited for any sign of movement. The boulder below hid the shooter, but Cole was sure the man cowered behind it, so he trained the barrel in line. With his eyes on the massive rock, his concentration was torn to his left by the impact of lead against stone and the whir of a spinning slug.

The missed shot came from the left. The unmistakable sound of a Winchester echoed three times. He'd been flanked, but he couldn't see by who. With a glance down, he saw the last of the riders turning the bend in the canyon. Hastings was the sole hope of stopping this rider from coming from behind and up the sloped escarpment. Cole didn't like being trapped.

Again he rolled back to sight the boulder. The shooter from behind it rose and shouldered a rifle. Cole fired. The bullet nicked the top of the boulder and the shooter once again crouched for cover. With one attacker pinned down, Cole pumped the action and fired. When the bullet again scraped the boulder, he again fired, pumped, and fired once more, rising to a knee to get a better angle.

A Winchester shot came from the left. Reflex drooped the Mouton rifle from Cole's shoulder. He pumped the action and pulled the trigger. The bullet sailed high and harmless. The panicked attacker levered the Winchester. Cole pumped the Mouton. The Winchester fired first.

The slug hit in front of Cole. Stone chips peppered his left hand, jolting the Mouton rifle from his grasp and forcing him onto his back. The attacker quickly fired again. The bullet whirred over Cole's head. The attacker levered the Winchester for another shot. Cole drew the Colt, pulled back the hammer, and fired wildly.

The pistol shot startled the attacker and his shot went wild. Cole fired again. White smoke clouded his view for an instant. He pulled back the hammer while pulling the .36 from the coat with his left hand. He fired the Colt, then pulled the trigger on the .36. As the white smoke cleared, he saw the attacker charge toward him, Winchester at the shoulder.

A rifle shot struck the rock next to Cole's left ear. As rapidly as his fingers could cock hammers and pull triggers, he sent as much lead as he had toward the figure holding the rifle. Smoke and blasts filled the air around them. As he fired, he tensed every muscle, waiting for a slug to tear into him.

Hammers fell on empty shells. After more cocking and pulling to only the sound of hollow clicks, the smoke finally cleared from view. The attacker lay face first on the rocks not ten feet away, blood streaming from under his head and chest.

Cole sucked in air, trying to sustain normal breath. A bullet crashed into the rock to the right. It came from the shooter below. Rolling onto his shoulder, Cole crawled back behind suitable shelter from the gunfire. Richard emerged from his cowering pose.

Once out of the line of fire, Cole glanced at the Mouton rifle, which lay near the dead attacker and in range of the man behind the boulder. Cole flicked open the Colt's chamber gate with his right thumb, then placed the pistol in his left palm.

"We've got to find that rider. Keep him from coming up here."

With his right fingers, he rolled the cylinder. One by one, the spent shells dropped from the pistol as he popped six fresh cartridges from his belt loops.

"You're going to have to go down there and find him."

When the cylinder was empty, he angled the Colt down and without pause inserted a new shell into each hole while rolling the cylinder clockwise.

"Me?" Richard questioned.

Cole nodded, snapping the chamber gate shut on the Colt and snugging it into the holster. He unlatched the breech on the .36 and dug in his pocket for bullets.

"I'll keep them busy with me, but if that rider comes up from the rear and we take fire from both him and at the front," he said with a shake of the head as he slid in the last shell, "we're done for."

It took a moment for Richard to nod his understanding. He inhaled deeply. "All right."

Cole cocked the hammers of both pistols, then looked into the eyes of his young friend. "Don't give him a chance. You see him, you shoot him. Dead." Slowly, he edged an eye up to see the canyon floor. "Go."

Richard waddled down the sloping escarpment in a crouch. As the reporter descended, Cole moved farther, keeping watch of the boulder. His view twisted from down, to right, to eyeing the Mouton rifle lying to the left. To risk retrieval might bring further fire, but the better weapon was worth the gamble. With both revolvers pointed below, he sidestepped closer.

As before, he kept watch of the boulder, snatching a glimpse over his shoulder. Richard was gone from view. Gunshots erupted from the direction of the canyon mouth. It was too soon for Richard to have gotten that far. Maybe Hastings had met up with the rider. Cole saw that the shooter below was caught in the same confusion.

Both men hesitated together, then, without cover to hide, Cole fired the Colt. The bullet hit the boulder. Again, he fired the Colt and the .36, to send the shooter back behind the rock. More fire came from farther up the canyon. Bullets whirred overhead, so he dove to stay prone. The Mouton rifle was too close to the edge to crawl and expose him as an easier target.

Wild shots with the Colt were no equal for rifle fire. After firing the .36 then cocking the Colt, he stopped pulling the trigger upon sighting the Winchester under the dead attacker.

The black smoke dissipated. Richard flinched from the frequent shooting at the mouth of the canyon below. He stayed in his crouch, hoping to keep unnoticed. Each blast of gunfire came with a puff of white smoke. It appeared the rider had taken shelter behind the surrounding rocks. By the angle of the gunsmoke, the shots were aimed at the opposite side of the mouth. Hastings must have been in those shrubs and rocks that lined the opening. Richard found himself behind the man he was to shoot.

He took the .45 in his grip. With the dense scrub clouding his view, he crept closer for a clear shot. The knowledge that he'd have only one chance to kill this man made him shake, so he closed his eyes and attempted to steady his breath. Finally certain in his mind, he crawled on elbows and knees farther down the slope.

The cadence of gunfire slowed. The closer he came, the more he noticed the absence of white smoke coming from the opposite side of the mouth. The thought of something happening to Hastings froze him stiff. Soon, as he had suspected would happen, the now-dismounted gunman slowly emerged from the brush.

Here was his chance. Still unnoticed, he held the advantage. Not more than fifty feet away stood the target. His heart raced; his fingers trembled, trying to raise the pistol. The man slowly walked toward the opposite side with his gun pointed in front. Since the target now moved, Richard gradually pushed himself to kneel and keep the barrel in line with what he hoped to hit.

However, this wasn't a "what," it was a "who." A man. Another human. One not posing a threat to his own life at the moment. One not even facing him. Was this murder? No. This man was a criminal. A killer himself. Richard tried to inhale to calm his nerves, but his chest wouldn't expand.

Unable to breathe, he forced himself to point the pistol at the walking target. His trembling hand wobbled the barrel. His shaking thumb pressed down the hammer. The stiff mechanism required more force. He pressed harder, but with no success. He increased the pressure, and the thumb slipped off the hammer. The weight of the revolver shifting forward jarred his grip. His sweaty palm couldn't hold the butt. The pistol spilled onto the rocks with a crash. The gunman twisted about with alarm and pointed his gun right at Richard.

In absolute panic, Richard raised his arms. "Don't shoot! Don't shoot!"

On his belly and with bullets pelting the edge of the escarpment, Cole crawled to the body sprawled on the rock. With his head low, he reached under the corpse and grasped the Winchester barrel. He yanked it loose, grabbed the bloody stock, and rolled on his back. A quick shove of the lever forward and the weapon was ready to fire.

Gradually, he inched up for a view of the shooter below. The lack of return fire encouraged the shooter to stray from the boulder. Once he saw Cole with the Winchester, the shooter dove for cover.

Cole pulled the trigger. The slug struck the man's leg. Another action on the lever ejected the empty shell and he loaded a fresh cartridge into the chamber and cocked the hammer. He sighted the barrel on the chest of the wounded quarry. Without hesitation, he closed his left eye and squeezed.

The bullet plunged through the center,

blood quickly staining the man's shirt.

Another ricochet from the left twisted Cole about. He levered and fired wild twice so as to cover the retrieval of the Mouton rifle and his retreat out of sight. He rolled shoulder over shoulder to the previous shelter spot. Unsure of the ammunition left in the Winchester, he paused, deciding whether to abandon the weapon.

"Rainmaker!"

The shout came from the direction of the last shot.

"Rainmaker, I got a friend of yours down here with me."

Cole said nothing, nor did he move.

"Are you hearing me? I said, I got a friend of yours with me. A fellow you want to see alive. Make sure he stays that way."

The tone increased, a sign the voice was moving. There was no reason to believe that if he showed himself he wouldn't attract more lead his way. Cole took both rifles and crept along the rear of the top of the rock. Slow and gradual, he made his way on the front edge, allowing him to peek down at the gang with their attention on his former position.

Inch by inch, he peeped over the edge. A stocky man walked step by step with the hostage as a shield. If not for the familiar clothes and black skin, he'd never have recognized Choate. The half-breed's once-burly frame now appeared thin and frail. Another rider cautiously led four horses behind. Every second that passed brought another step of the man with Choate. That one had to be Coy Dallas.

"You ain't going to be neighborly?" When they were even with the dead shooter on the ground, they hurried their pace. "Seems you haven't been neighborly with two of my men by my count. Maybe I ought to do the same with this one of yours?"

The threat quickly put the Mouton at the ready to fire. The constant movement of men and horses in the narrow canyon made for a risky shot. He eased away from his aim, fearing gunfire would claim Choate's life before it would the other two. Showing himself would likely draw the same result. Surrender wouldn't gain any more guarantees.

He watched as they went farther through the winding canyon. Once it appeared they thought it was safe, they mounted, loading Choate on the horse like a pack on a mule.

When they rounded the bend, Cole prowled the top of the escarpment. He had come too far to lose sight of them. When he passed the spot he and the greenhorn

269

reporter had first perched, his mind stopped him in place.

Where was Richard?

He ran to make up time. The escarpment sloped as it neared the canyon mouth. Despite the worry fueling his run, he couldn't cover the same distance as horses. Upon nearing the opening, he slowed his pace and crouched, placing the Winchester silently on the rocks and pointing the Mouton at the ready in case the riders still lingered.

In a slow approach, he came over the crest of the rock, viewing the sharp slope that led to the ground. He saw the opening. There were no riders and no sign of Richard. The absence of his friend pushed him a little faster down the slope, always ready to fire if fired upon.

However, there wasn't anyone in sight.

The bonfire of brush now was just wisps of embers. The more he descended, the less he was on guard. When he reached the ground, he knelt at the tracks at the opening. Five horses loaded with men and iron began a gallop at this point.

A rustle of brush on the far side of the opening drew his attention and the barrel of the Mouton. Poised to fire at an instant, he walked toward the noise. The brush was thick and as high as a man's height.

"Come on out. I'm a U.S. federal marshal."

A groan followed his call. "Marshal Hayes?"

The voice had a familiar cut. "Hastings?" The suspicion encouraged him to approach. When he poked the barrel into the brush and through the maze of small branches, the color red shone through. Cole charged into the stiff growth and finally forced his way next to the fallen mountie. A bullet had torn through the shoulder of the tunic. "What happened?"

Hastings strained to talk. "One of them came out. I called for him to stop." He winced. "But he began shooting instead."

The slow details frustrated Cole. "Where's Richard? Where's that kid?"

Hastings writhed with Cole's tug of the coat. "Don't pull. Don't pull."

"Damn you, tell me. The slug don't even look to have gone clean through you. Only nicked the top. You'll live. Now, tell me. Is he dead?"

Gulping for breath, Hastings shook his head. "No. They took him. The one that shot me, the rider, he took him captive."

"Captive?" Disappointment in the reporter's ability to get the job done made Cole roll his eyes. He had sent the kid off to shoot the rider and the kid had managed to get himself caught. "Where did they head?" He helped the mountie sit.

"I couldn't be certain. To the west leads only to broken ground or to the mountains."

"That don't make no sense. Not this late in the summer," said Cole while looking at the shoulder wound. Blood soaked the tunic, but the flow wasn't steady. "What's to the north?"

"The same as what you see. Calgary is two days away."

Cole peered in that direction. "What's there?"

"More men like me," Hastings answered with a crack of a smile. "There is a fort there to keep the peace between the Indian tribes and the ranchers."

"Where is it?"

The mountie answered with a grunt. "Where the Bow and the Elbow Rivers join."

The idea didn't seem sound. "He ain't going there. If I were him, I'd keep clear of any law I knew was around. Where else is there open range? Water?"

The question lingered while Hastings inhaled heavily. "I suppose he would go to northeast. But it will be twenty miles before you will find flat prairie."

Cole looked over his shoulder. The rock hills surrounded every line of sight. "Where are the horses?"

"I sent them scattered when the rider approached."

Cole nodded and curled his lips. He lifted Hastings to stand amid anguished groans. "Come on. We've got to find the rest of them. I don't think they could get too far in these rocks." He swung the rifle like an ax to cut their path through the growth.

"What are you going to do?" asked the mountie.

"I'm going to set you on your horse once we find them. I've got nothing to mend the wound here. You'll have to make it to nearest place you can get help." They marched through the brush and emerged at the canyon opening. "If you make it to your fort, send back as many as you can."

"And what about you?"

"I've got to pick up their tracks."

Chapter Fifteen

Dallas rode at the front. The thin patches of land between one rock-filled range and another galled him. It had been a long time since he traveled these parts, but memory served that soon open ground would be before him. With his horse at a lather and the sun angling farther west, he spotted an arroyo surrounded by high rocks. It was similar to one he'd just left, and he feared the same result, but it was the best place in the desired direction. He steered toward the narrow gap and those behind followed.

"What are we stopping here for?" asked Hix, pulling up his horse riding double with the stranger he'd caught.

Dallas dismounted. "Give these horses an hour rest. Then we'll set out after dark." As he watched Clem bring in the darkie and yank him from the saddle, curiosity set in about the young fellow dressed in dusty city clothes. Desperation and the anger of being near shot to death made him march up to the stranger and shove him to the dust. "Who are you?" he demanded while drawing his pistol and aiming square between the eyes.

"Richard Johnson" was the squeaky dry reply. "I don't have a gun. Please don't point that at me."

Dallas knelt next to Richard and spoke through gritted teeth. "Well, Richard Johnson, why are you here? What part do you have in this?"

After several deep breaths, the kid spoke in a pleading tone. "I am a reporter. A writer. I'm not the law. I just came for the adventure. I mean, the experience of seeing the West."

"Ain't the law?" Dallas paused to glance at Hix and Clem, then back at Richard. "There's a marshal out there. Seems he's the law. If you're not part of the posse, then what are you doing with him?"

Richard, too, eyed the others. He cast a quick glance at the black man who'd been pushed against the rock wall. The man appeared emaciated. The thought of the same fate crept into Richard's mind. For some reason, the truth sounded like the best tactic to pursue. "Like I said, I am a reporter for *Harper's Weekly*. It is a newspaper in New

York City." He took more deep breaths and looked into the faces of the outlaws in front of him. "I came west to find out about . . ." He paused, bringing his eyes to the front, where he stared deeply into the cold heart of Coy Dallas. Suddenly, fiction appeared a more powerful advantage. "To find out about a famous man of the West. A man named Coy Dallas."

Dallas backed away in surprise. "Me?"

Richard nodded, realizing he'd struck upon something. "Of course. You're very well known in the East. People want to know more about you. So I came here to learn as much as I could. When the chance came to actually speak to you, I eagerly seized the opportunity."

"That's a damn lie," said Hix. "The son of a bitch was going to shoot me in the back."

"No," Richard answered with palms open. "I surrendered my weapon." He panted in panic. "I could have shot you, but I did not. I knew that if I surrendered I would have a better chance to meet Mr. Dallas."

With a look of question, Dallas rose and glared at Richard, pointing the pistol and cocking the hammer. "Are you lying to us, boy?"

It took a gulp to slow his beating heart and steady his voice, but he couldn't keep his eyes from the gun aimed at him. Richard averted his view to the ground. "No." All there was to do now was close his eyes and wait.

The click of the hammer made him flinch. However, when he felt no pain associated with the noise, he dared to open his eyes and peer up. Dallas had eased the hammer uncocked and tucked the pistol into his holster. "So who is this marshal shooting at us? Is it this man called the Rainmaker I heard about?"

Since the question was asked with a civil tone, he tried to answer in an appropriate manner. He grunted his throat clear of the mucus. "Yes. It is."

"How many men does he have with him?"

The threat of the pistol being drawn again forced him to revert to the truth. "He's by himself. There's a Canadian Mounted Policeman with him also."

"That the one I killed?" Hix asked.

The inquiry had the effect of a shuddering announcement. "You killed him?"

Hix grinned. "Hell, I hope so. I unloaded six bullets in his direction. I think I'm a better shot than missing all six." The remark brought laughter, but only for a moment.

"So what are we waiting around for?" Clem asked. "Morton and Harper are dead. Let's do the same to these two as payback for our friends and hightail it out of here."

"Hush your mouth," ordered Dallas. "I give the orders here." He pointed at the black man. "I told you it'd do good to keep this nig around. He's the reason we made it out of that canyon." His attention turned to Richard. "Now we got two reasons to keep that marshal off us." A bob of the head signaled an address. "What you think? Is your Rainmaker going to keep after us?"

Perhaps it was time for a logical approach. "I believe he will come." He paused only long enough to glance at the black man. "As long as you hold two of his friends."

"So what are you saying?" Dallas again knelt in a casual manner and pushed back his hat above his balding scalp. "You and him really friends? Him and this nig here? That's all he wants?"

The choice of words made him pause. Richard sensed that Dallas was truly considering releasing the both of them. He saw a way to escape with his life and answered with vigor. "Yes, of course. It is the entire reason he's come this far. I'm sure he would allow you to go about your way should you turn us loose."

As was his habit, Dallas glanced at the other two outlaws. The action appeared as a silent question being asked. After having held Hix's face for more than ten seconds, it sparked a reply.

"Don't make no difference to me, Coy. I'd soon turn the both of them loose and be rid of them. I didn't want to bring that nig this far, nohow. If it means we can be on our way, then set them free and let's be done with it."

Richard breathed with ease for the first time all day, hoping his plan would have the desired effect. However, his hope was short-lived, because Clem barked an opinion.

"That would be damn stupid. Coy is right. Keeping him with us stopped the lead from coming. We let them go, then they'll open fire without stopping."

"Didn't help Harper none. Morton neither," Hix replied with spite. "When I was out front by myself taking fire, it was them two that covered me."

Clem didn't show any concern for the complaint. "It was your turn. We've all had to take one."

"I didn't see you out there yet, Clem." Hix pointed at the black man. "I wasn't the one hiding behind him."

"Hush your mouths, the both of you."

Dallas's order put an instant stop to the bickering. The leader again turned his attention to Richard. "Who is this man? This Rainmaker? All I've heard is a bunch of talk. But it can't all be true. What's his name?"

"Truth be known, I don't know that much about him. It is said that he was with Custer at the time of the slaughter, but I'm beginning to believe that is just legend." The hope that freedom was coming soon faded. More needed to be said to convince Dallas. "I've personally seen him kill four men. The two of your friends included. Three, if you count the man behind the Gatling gun as one of your own."

"Tanner," Hix said with a ghostly tone.

"Tanner? He killed Jeff Tanner?"

Richard nodded. Like a shroud of gloom, the deeds of the Rainmaker hung over these men's dwindling confidence before his very eyes. Instead of a negotiated truce, it was apparent that spreading seeds of doubt might lead to an outright capitulation.

"Killed him dead. Shot him right through the heart at greater than a hundred yards."

"I told you," Hix said with some satisfaction. "It was the best shot I ever seen."

Dallas didn't seem impressed by his man's endorsement. He glared at Hix. "Enough for you to turn tail like a woman, leaving

Tanner there to die."

"Tanner was dead when he hit the ground, like I said. There was nothing I could do. I couldn't help him anymore, and it wouldn't help you if I was killed, too."

The explanation didn't wear into the leader's scowl.

"So, what's his name?" he asked Richard.

There seemed little harm in telling the truth. "He's Clay Cole."

"I heard of him," said Clem, turning all attention his way. "When I was in prison, I heard that name talked about. He's a buff hunter, or was at one time." Clem looked to Richard almost in an attempt to discredit the ominous reputation. "He's a coward. A traitor. Heard he was a scout for the cavalry. The army is out to hang him for betraying Custer. He turned yellow and has run ever since."

"That's not the whole story," Richard said to counter the remarks. "Not all is known about that. Besides, I've been with this man. He is no coward." Richard looked deep into Dallas's eyes. "I happen to know he was a personal friend of the legendary pistoleer Wild Bill Hickok."

The attempt to instill awe dissolved with the speed of melting snow on a summer's day. Although slow in forming, Dallas's grin broke into a wide guffaw. "Hickok? Hickok was nothing but a drunken gambler who killed men he owed money to." The insult brought more laughter. "Most of them he shot in the back. He got what was coming to him in Deadwood."

Richard took offense and felt obligated to take up for the legend. "He was a feared man. Yes, he did gamble, as many do. But no man ever garnered the same respect as a pistoleer. He killed two men in duels."

"They were drunk. He was just less so."

"He was acquitted of all charges." Despite his attempt, these men weren't believers. "He was an Indian fighter. A sheriff in Kansas cowtowns. He stood up against Texas cowboys by himself."

"Didn't he kill his own deputy doing it?" asked Clem with a chuckle. "That's why he was alone." Louder laughter erupted.

"If Hickok is the best pair you can draw to this Clay Cole, then I ain't too worried." The laughter continued until Richard dared remind them of the day's events.

"You're forgetting about the men he killed. What were their names? Harper? Morton? Tanner?"

The giddy mood faded. Dallas's scowl returned within a blink. "That he did. And I aim to make it up to him. Let him know just who it is he's dealing with." He gave only a quick glance at his remaining men. "You say he's out alone, did you? Well, he shouldn't be too hard to find."

"I didn't say he was alone."

"All there was with him was a mountie. Hix turned him dead. That leaves just this Rainmaker." Slowly he drew his revolver. "Unless you've been lying to us all this time. Have you, Richard? You been lying to me?"

With a cold steel muzzle to stare at, it was no time to embellish. "No." His stomach churned with the words. Words to be used to plot against Cole, and maybe his own life. "He's by himself."

The wry grin returned. "That's what I thought." Dallas stood and turned to Hix and Clem. "Change of plans, boys. We're going to stay here and wait him out. Start a fire. We'll cook a little supper before night-fall, then we'll put it out. Can't make it that easy for him to find us."

The two subordinates didn't appear to agree with their leader. However, they complied by moving the horses farther out of sight from the grassy ground. While the gang prepared the camp, Richard seized the opportunity to inch closer to the black man.

"Are you Choate?" he whispered. The answer was slow in coming, only a feeble blink. A verbal response was unlikely. "My God, they haven't given you anything to eat, have they?" A wary glance told him that the men had not noticed him talking. "Have faith. He will find us." The encouragement had no effect on the black man's face. His features showed fatigue, and he appeared ready to faint at any moment. Richard leaned closer. "Hold on."

CHAPTER SIXTEEN

Daylight seeped between Richard's eyelids. When his eyes were fully open, he saw the same surroundings he'd left the previous night only now by morning's light. With his back against a rock wall, he lay in shadow with the rocks above him bathed in cloudless sunlight.

A glance to the left showed Choate still asleep. He hoped it was only the exhaustion he saw and not the grip of death. Upon closer inspection, he observed the faint motion of Choate's nostrils.

Dallas and his men chewed on some food of undetermined origin while readying their equipment. It reminded Richard of his own hunger. Another glance at Choate reinforced the idea that these captors were unconcerned with their hostages' health. Despite his own growling stomach, he gathered the courage to ask on Choate's behalf. "I think he needs food. He may die."

The request got Dallas's attention. "He's been that way for more than two weeks now." An evil grin creased his face. "He can last a little longer."

The statement seemed to refer to a final destination. "Where are you taking us?"

The evil grin widened. "That depends on your friend out there. You may be going with him."

"Really?" The possibility seemed too good to be true. "What do you want? In return for letting us go?"

"Depends what he's got." With the vague reply, Dallas turned his head to the other two men. "Clem, give me a hand here." The subordinate complied, walking toward his boss.

"Up there," Hix shouted, pointing above. "Look. That's him." All eyes were drawn to a distant hill. At the top, a figure stood. Richard squinted, trying to focus. Barely, he made out a black hat, dark shirt, and lighter-pigmented pants. His heart beat quicker as a warm wave ran through him from head to toe.

"I'll be damned," muttered Dallas. Clem slowly raised his rifle to the shoulder, cocking the hammer and closing one eye. Dallas grabbed the barrel. "Don't waste a shot. He's out of range." A grin broke his face; he appeared pleased at the discovery. "He's one smart fellow. He knows we seen him but can't do nothing about it. Too far away to talk to. So to do any talking or shooting, we're going to have get closer to him."

The figure stayed in place for more than a minute. Suddenly, it turned around and left the crest of the hill, descending out of sight on the far side.

"Clem, you and Hix go after him."

"Why us?" Clem complained. "What are you going to do?"

Dallas's grin vanished. "Do what I tell you. Don't you see? He's after them two. If we run, he'll follow. It's best to put an end to this now. You both surround him from each side and close in. That will flush him my way. Between the three of us, we'll kill him for sure and be done with this whole business."

"What if he don't come this way?" Hix said, worried. "Remember, he has that damn rifle that shoots farther than these repeaters."

"That's why both of you go," replied Dallas in an agitated tone. "Hell, I thought the both of you were men. This is just like hunting a cougar. When you flank him on one side, he'll go to the other. You keep him pinned in the middle. If he doubles back behind you, he's got to come toward me."

"And where will you be?"

"Right here," he said with his grin returning. "Waiting on him."

Both Clem and Hix stood, a mixture of frustration and fear etched on their faces. Dallas motioned for them to be on their way, and after a few moments, they ran to opposite sides of the massive rock wall.

Richard watched as the two men departed, then his eyes switched to the sly grin of Coy Dallas. He picked cartridges from his pocket and slid them into the loader slot of his Winchester. "Now we'll see how he likes being hunted," Dallas said.

More than ten minutes passed before Hix climbed to the top of the rocky wall. He stared at the long incline of solid stone ahead of him. The Rainmaker was nowhere in sight. Neither was Clem. Accepting the possibility that he'd gotten to the top first, he went forward in a crouch, nervously twisting his head left and right for any sign of movement.

As he moved, his mind nagged at him as to why he'd been sent. When he had joined the outfit, he had sought the promised bounty of ten thousand a man. Tanner was the one who made the promise, but now he was dead. Coy Dallas seemed concerned more with killing folks than raiding trains and robbing banks for fat mine payrolls. He himself had no quarrel with the folks being killed, but when the leader of the gang wants them dead, it's wise to follow so as to be paid.

His shadow preceded him. Halfway up the incline, he slowed his pace, constantly eyeing the crest, ready at any moment to drop and fire. However, there was only silence each time he stopped. Again he scanned to the right. Still there was no Clem.

A moment's thought of waiting or even signaling faded quickly. The longer he waited, the easier a target he was to hit. With a gulp, he continued up.

The steep jagged rocks slowed Clem. He climbed one secure step at a time, pausing after each one to see if his approach had been noticed. He cringed with each rustle of pebbles and dust sliding, but there was only the hill above him.

If he had his horse, he would ride to the rear of the hill and approach there. A second thought convinced him that it would take half the day to ride that far and at least as long to climb where he needed. A third thought crept into his mind. If he did have his horse, he might keep on riding. Even if it meant going back to prison.

Dallas had proved true what was said about him. The bandit had gone plumb loco. Although Jeff Tanner had some strange ideas, they were mite concerns compared to the leader's. If he were able to do it over, he'd refuse the lure of money. Now he was on the side of a giant hill a thousand miles from home, facing down death.

After another step, his foot slipped, sending him sliding on his belly several feet. Once he stopped the slide, the sizzling noise of dust falling steered his focus to the top of the hill.

There he stood at the top. The Rainmaker. Rifle in his hands.

In reflex to the threat, Clem instantly tried to aim, but his rifle had been jarred from his grasp and lay out of reach just feet ahead of him. For a single second he expected to be shot dead, but the Rainmaker made no move to shoot. He used the momentary reprieve to scramble after the fallen Winchester. Once it was in his grip, he cocked the hammer and pointed it up. The Rainmaker was gone.

He rose to his feet in panic and charged up the hill, the rifle stock at his shoulder and prepared to fire. The farther he strode, the steeper the incline and the heavier the strain on his legs. The unstable footing wobbled his balance, forcing him to dip his eyes down to be sure of his next step, always in fear of a bullet coming at him. The loose stones provided no cover. To stop could get him killed.

Each breath stabbed his side, but he dare not stop. With every three steps, he glanced upward. He ran bobbing to the left and the right so as to not give the Rainmaker a steady line on him. His attempt to keep as long a watch upward as possible caused him to misstep, and he tripped, his knees going into the hard stones. Pain shot through him. He closed his eyes, writhing from the impact. When he opened them, there stood the Rainmaker.

He shouldered his weapon, but the Rainmaker again dipped from sight. Clem couldn't stop from pulling the trigger.

Hix flinched when he heard the shot and instinct brought him to his knees. The familiar sound was that of a Winchester, but the echo made determining the direction from where it came difficult.

Clem shot the Rainmaker? Or was Clem dead?

He shook the questions from his mind.

The only real way to know any answers was to get to the apex of the hill. He took another gulp and resumed his careful stalk, only now he kept his Winchester poised and ready to fire.

A blur of black and green jutted into view above. Bullets ricocheted off the rocks in the front, followed by two loud booming echoes. Hix fell to his belly. To stop further shots, he rose to his knees and fired, but the slug hit nothing, not stone or man. As he clumsily levered the rifle, the Rainmaker ran along the top of the rocks. The sight of his prey in full view made him hesitate an instant. By the time he had put a bullet in the chamber and fired wild, the Rainmaker had again dipped behind the crest of the hill.

Hix rose to his feet and ran, seizing the chance to fire again. While on the run, he levered the stiff action once more. A few feet from the crest, he collapsed to his knees so as to not expose himself to a crouched shooter. On elbows and knees, he crept to the crest. He peeked over the edge and saw more rocks and hills, but no man.

Five gunshots seized Clem stiff. The initial blast seemed to come from Hix's side of the hill before the echo clamored in all directions. Another glance to the crest gave him confidence to resume the charge to the top. As he neared, he kept the muzzle aimed in front, the hammer back and ready to blow a hole in the first thing he saw.

More hills came into view. Grassy valleys and a winding stream lay far beyond. Farther to the left, another mountain range rose from the horizon. He quickly glanced over his shoulder and saw the snowcaps stretching into the sky. What he sought wasn't in view; the man shooting at him.

As he searched, he heard a rustling scratch to the left. Cautious, Clem crept at a crouch, the Winchester pointed ahead and ready to fire. The farther he went, the more distinct the noise. Sure he would find what he wanted, he raised the weapon to his shoulder. Each step revealed more of what lay over the far side of the hill. A last step showed a figure lying prone. He poised his finger to fire.

"Hold off," screamed Hix. The shout saved his life. Clem lowered his rifle and drooped his shoulders.

"Damn, Hix. I nearly put a bullet in you."

Hix waved to get low. Clem did so and crawled next to him. "Keep your voice down." He pointed to the valley below. "He's down there somewhere. I chased him to that spot."

"Are you sure?"

"Hell, yes, I'm sure. He ran right in front of me. Shot at me twice and I fired two back at him."

Clem shook his head in exasperation. "I did, too. I came up from the far side. I lost my footing and dropped my gun." He inhaled rapidly as fear etched his face. "He had me cold dead. Could have killed me easy, but he didn't. Gave me time to pick up my rifle, and then he was gone."

Hix nodded. "Had the same thought myself. I heard the shots. He came back at me. Him having the higher ground, I thought he could hit me for sure. But he fired short."

"So why do you think he's doing this?" Clem asked almost in a pant.

"Don't know." Hix turned his attention back down the valley. "But chasing him is taking us further away from Coy."

"Yeah," Clem agreed. "Like some sort of injun trick."

"Could be." Hix leaned to his right, but he couldn't see anything more at that angle. "I'm going to go down there from the left. You go right." Slowly, he rose to his knees. "Be ready to shoot." Once Clem finally gave a nod, Hix got on his feet and went down the rock slope. After a few steps, he glanced back. Clem had started his descent.

With a slight lean to the rear, Hix pulled the hammer back on the rifle. Gravity pulled him faster than he wanted to go. He angled a glimpse of Clem, who slid on his boot soles trying to stop. Soon both of them were below the height of the tops of the tall firs growing in the valley.

When the two came off the rocks and onto the dirt, they quickly searched behind the near trees but found no one. They looked to each other. Clem shrugged. Hix turned his attention to the rim of the rocky bluff now above them. He took a breath and silently chided himself. They had just traded the high ground for the low.

He waved to Clem and both went farther to the left along the base of the rocks. Rifles at the front, they cautiously went around every bend and jagged edge of the large boulders, each time finding no sign of anyone.

"Where is he?" Clem asked.

Hix shook his head. "I don't know." After a few heavy breaths, he pointed along the base. "You go down this line. I'll go up. Keep me in sight, and I'll do the same for you." When Clem nodded, they both went along the two parallel paths.

As before, they proceeded only one carefully placed step at a time. Hix twisted his head to each side and back, looking for any motion. While scanning about, he caught sight of a black object. Instinct made him freeze, but he was able to lock his eyes on what he saw high in the rocks: a black hat just under a precipice extending out the far side in the stone hill.

Without a sound, he raised his hand to signal Clem. When he had his partner's attention, he pointed at the hat above, then motioned for the two of them to approach on opposite sides of the hat. Clem nodded his understanding and began to walk up the steep incline.

Hix had his finger wrapped around the trigger ready to fire, his chest tight with anticipation. As he neared, the muzzle of a rifle came into view. He stopped stiff, but when the weapon didn't move at their approach, he felt they still held the advantage.

Carefully, he stepped to the side to widen his view, but the hat was low to the line of sight. He couldn't see a head. Still, he ascended, his Winchester poised at his shoulder. He glanced at Clem, who also was prepared to let go of lead in a hurry. Within sight of the barrel poking up from the rocks, Hix charged up the hill. Clem responded in kind.

When they came around the precipice, both took dead aim at the hat and rifle, but there was no man, no body.

Hix stood as if he'd been hollowed out inside. His hands trembled, wanting to pull the trigger, but better sense held his finger firm.

"Where is he?" Clem asked in frustration.

Straining for breath, Hix couldn't speak, able only to shake his head. Sunlight glared off the white rock hill on the far slope. He angled his palm to shield his eyes. Slowly, he focused on a shaded butte across from a small ravine.

A chill ran through him when he heard a man shout.

"Drop your weapons!"

CHAPTER SEVENTEEN

Crouched in the shadows, Cole aimed the Mouton at the pair. When neither complied, he repeated his order. "Drop your weapons, or I'll kill you where you stand." He recognized the one in the black vest and checkered shirt as the point rider from the canyon. The other was the one who had held the horses while Dallas pointed a gun at Choate.

He didn't want to kill them, at least not just yet, but his hope of bartering for the lives of Choate and Richard with these two was fading fast. It was a rough gamble, but if he could capture these two, he might have a chance.

His demand stood unheeded. He fired a shot off the precipice to scare them into surrender. The ploy failed. The two both returned fire and ducked behind cover.

Cole pumped the action and fired, but his shot missed. When he pumped again, the trigger didn't arm. The magazine in the rifle was empty. He slid the bolt back, releasing the cartridge holder to fall on the rocks. Quickly, he drew his last magazine and inserted it into the hole at the bottom of the rifle, slammed the bolt forward, and pumped a shell into the chamber.

The time it took to reload allowed the black vest to advance to the lower rocks while the other fired blind. The hail of bullets crashing off the rocks around him forced Cole to seek better cover. He moved left where the rubble of the butte provided a better shield. Once set, he saw the black vest at the bottom of the ravine. Cole fired once, the shot striking the rocks near his target, pumped, and prepared to shoot again. His finger seized still. He had only eight cartridges left in this last magazine. The next one had to find its mark.

The other shooter fired every time Cole rose to gain a better angle at the black-vested attacker. Although he himself was hidden in shadow, the glare off the far hill made it hard for him to line up the sights. When another shot rippled the air, Cole looked to the puff of smoke and shot.

Dust from his bullet plumed into the air. He ejected the spent shell and looked to the approaching attacker below. Again he rose slightly to get a better aim. Revealing his position brought fire from the far right. Cole sank behind the rocks.

"Coy, that you?" echoed off the rocks.

"Yeah. I can keep him down from here. You go on ahead."

Now with three shooters against him, Cole needed to slow their advance. He edged just above his cover and fired once. The one in the black vest stopped short of fifty yards away. The distance was no challenge, but pinned down from two other angles kept him from aiming.

If he was to make a stand, he had to lessen the shooters against him. He couldn't see Dallas on the far right, and with the black vest already behind the rocks, the best chance he had was to stay in his crouch and aim at the one still in the glare.

He propped the Mouton on the rocks and squinted an eye. The light continued to distort the view, but if he drew the prey out with a single shot, he might goad a return shot where he could line up his sights. With his chances slipping, he squeezed the trigger. The same spray of dust appeared as before.

Two Winchester replies rippled back. The gunsmoke was clear. Cole targeted the plumes. He fired, pumping the action, firing again. When he pumped a third time, an agonized wail made him hold from his third shot. Squinting into the distance, he barely saw a red hue now streaming down from the top of the far hill.

A bullet smashed the rocks in front of him, sending jagged bits of stone at him like the spread of buckshot. A piece as big as his palm crashed into his forehead, and smaller pieces pelted his nose and cheeks.

He fell on his back, pain whirling his head like a twister. The warm taste of blood trickled into his lips. While he writhed he tried to inhale. A stab to his nose sent a bolt of lightning through his nerves. Through the agony, he knew his nose was broken.

The sound of loud footsteps crunching over the loose stones crept into his ears. It had to be the one in the black vest approaching at a run. With blood clouding his vision, dizziness confusing his head, the only tactic left to him was playing possum.

He rolled onto his right side to hide as much of his injured face as possible and shield his gun hand. If he could get a few seconds' time to recover, he might fend off the attackers. The footsteps grew louder. Soon he heard a man's breathing. Cole let his body go limp.

Eyes closed, he concentrated on every sound. Any click of gunmetal and he would have to roll back over and shoot blind. The footsteps stopped. Every second that passed seemed like hours.

"Looks like you got him, Coy," came as a loud shout just over Cole's ear.

"Are you sure?" echoed back.

Cole tensed, ready to spring at the first signal of a gun being aimed his way. A hand gripped his shoulder. He held his breath and let his body slump, but only to allow himself to be rolled on his shoulders, keeping his hand tucked beneath his hip for a quick grip of the Colt.

The foul stench of the man's breath wafted into his face, but he remained motionless. Fingers clutched his jaw. Cole let it fall ajar. Cole remained relaxed, hoping to fool the man inches above him, but ready to raise the pistol to the man's ribs.

"Yeah" was yelled. "He's dead. Looks to be shot right through the nose." A hearty laugh followed, like a celebration of the killing.

Moments passed, but Cole sensed the man still above him. His lungs begged for air, but he wasn't sure where the eyes of his attacker were aimed. Creeping his eyelids up, he saw two legs straddling his body, but to see any more would require him to open his eyelids fully. The risk was too great.

His lungs were ready to burst and inhale greatly, so he decided he had to shoot. He wrapped his fingers around the butt and trigger of the Colt. As he was about to draw the revolver, a loud blast rang out.

The noise instantly seized his muscles. He felt no pain. Had he been shot? Was he dead? Was his body too numb to feel the agony of the bullet?

Less than a second later, a heavy weight collapsed atop him. The slam of the weight and his reflex to it jarred his head, sending the same pain shooting through his nose. When he cringed, he opened his eyes and prepared to shoot. However, his arm was pinned beneath the body of the man with the black vest.

Still shielded by the rocks and the motionless body, Cole remained still for several minutes. When he gained confidence that Dallas had given him up for dead, he slid from under the black-vested attacker.

The pain in his nose made it hard for him to focus, but the bloody hole through the center of the forehead of the black-vested attacker made it clear what had happened. Dallas had ended all partnerships in the gang.

Slowly he edged an eye over the rocks. He blotted the blood from his face with his sleeve to see. There wasn't any motion in the ravine. No noise of any activity. A concentrated stare across the ravine and up to the precipice on the high hill confirmed that his shot had found its mark.

Even though he was alone in the rocks, the pain pounding his nose, face, and head sapped the strength he needed to pursue Dallas. It took several minutes before he garnered the inner courage to put his fingers on each side of his nose. Despite anguished torment as he listened to the crackle of bone, he pushed it straight and was able to breathe through it again. He lay back down and breathed heavy to let the pain subside. He needed rest for the long walk back to the palomino.

Richard's attention was turned to the left. The rustle of stones and dust was soon followed by the emergence of Dallas from between the rocks. Questions flooded his mind.

"What happened? I heard gunshots."

Dallas ignored the questions and in a determined way assembled his gear and saddled his horse.

"Where are Hix and Clem?"

"They ain't coming back." The answer was

sure, swift, and without remorse.

Richard closed his eyes and forced the next question from his lips. "What about Clay Cole?"

"Dead, too." It was the same matter-of-fact response.

Richard hung his head. In a normal world, he would express his grief at the loss of a friend, despite having known him for just a short time. However, he couldn't afford any more concern than that he held for his own welfare. He lifted his head and observed Dallas. Even though the conflict appeared over, Dallas continued his effort with diligent urgency. Richard feared there were still matters left to deal with. He glanced at the slumping Choate, then back at Dallas. "What are you planning next?"

The inquiry stopped Dallas. He turned, drew a folding knife from his pocket, and approached. Richard's eyes widened, wondering if he had sparked the suggestion of his own demise. Instead, Dallas sliced through the twine binding his hands to Choate's. Standing above, Dallas folded the knife shut and ordered in a direct tone, "Get him on a horse."

"We're leaving? Where are we going?"

"You let me worry about that." He went back to preparing his saddle to ride. Richard rose to his feet, and his legs wobbled and ached as blood slowly flowed through the muscles that had been deprived so long. Hunger stabbed at his gut, but he didn't press the issue for fear of stoking Dallas's temper.

Instead, he helped Choate up. The black man now resembled more a sack of bones. Gradually, Choate was able to open his eyes. Richard supported the man's weight by putting his arms under the man's shoulders, giving him a chance to whisper.

"Clay is dead." The black man's eyes opened gradually. Richard nodded discreetly to affirm the truth. "We're on our own."

CHAPTER EIGHTEEN

The terrain rose and fell like huge waves frozen stiff in place. Gray clouds hung close to the hilly ground. Grass swayed in the breeze, first one way, then the other. Cole dismounted and walked carefully over the rocks and boulders poking out from the dirt. If there were tracks around to follow, they'd not be easy to spot.

He came to the edge of a small bluff, looking out at the endless range to the north. The wind held the snap of winter soon to come. A gust dipped his head to the side. An unusual black shape against the brown rocks and yellowing grass caught his attention. He blinked twice to focus and to be sure what he saw wasn't to make a bigger fool of himself. The longer he stared, the more square the shape appeared.

He'd allow the palomino to graze while he cautiously descended the jagged rocky point. Once the few footholds were gone, he decided to jump the remaining feet rather than be blown off by the wind. The sharp edges scraped his palms, but he shook the pain away, anxious to find out what he'd seen.

He was careful not to disturb too much for fear of missing another sign, and his eyes widened when he recognized the shape. Despite the increased wind, his chest went empty when he saw the leather-bound journal. He knelt to pick it from the dirt and flipped through the pages. The words were a jumble. Moisture had smeared the pencil lead. Those that weren't stained with drops didn't make any sense to him anyway. No matter what was written, it required reading for more clues as to where the reporter had gone.

The shine of the gold watch caught his eye. It lay where he had picked up the book, as if meant to be hidden. He popped back the clasp to open the cover and peered at the image of Richard's wife. She held a faithful smile, one that tore at Cole's gut as he thought of what that smile would turn to upon her learning of her husband's fate. He let out a breath and closed his eyes for an instant. When he opened them, he noticed the hands of the watch.

Both hands pointed at the two. Unsure

why it even drew his notice, he looked to the sky. The dim light seeping through the clouds made it hard for him to determine the actual time of day, but the idea of so many hours passing since dawn of this day didn't seem right. Maybe he really couldn't sense the time as Richard had dared him. He paused there on a knee and pondered why this situation appeared so odd.

There was no doubt that the watch and book belonged to Richard. The fact that they were left behind didn't seem unusual, although there was no sign of a camp. The high grass hid tracks, especially with the swirling breeze. As he wondered if he should take more notice, he saw the motionless second hand of the watch. If it had stopped due to not being wound, then it must have been more than a day since it was left.

Confused, he rose and walked farther into the grass. When he looked closer, a pattern of bent stems and blades showed that shod horses had traveled through them. A hundred feet farther, he saw the same signs. He looked off to the west where the tracks seemed to lead. He hoped he was wrong.

The mountains were to the west. Snow deeper than twenty feet had already built up by this time of year, with plenty more on the way. If he was to chase them farther up higher ground, without the benefit of ample supplies, it wouldn't be long before he started to spot the remains of the party. That was if he himself didn't succumb to the elements. He again hung his head.

Once more he found himself staring at the watch in his hand. He didn't want to believe what the signs were telling him. The longer he thought about what next to do, the more something seemed out of place. The stem plumb was raised.

He pressed the stem down and the second hand immediately moved. Young Richard was a stickler for accuracy. His perky questions about the time were an annoyance, but now they may have been sending him a message. Why would he leave the watch and why would he stop the time? As soon as he asked himself the question, the answer was clear.

Both hands were pointed the same way. They pointed in the same direction. He recalled where he had found the timepiece, and where the hands would be pointed when he found it. He didn't need the wind to turn his head to the northeast.

Cole ran back to the bluff and climbed up the rocks to the top. It didn't take long to get to the palomino. He rode the short distance to where the ground evened with the plain where he had stood previously. About to turn to the northeast, he stopped the horse and looked back at the journal lying on the ground. Why he needed it he couldn't answer. However, if the watch was telling the truth, there might be something scrawled on the pages that could tell him more. Soon, he held it in his hand and steered the mount. At an amble, he flipped through the pages hoping for a sign, maybe a map, but there were only words. Words that he wished he understood. He closed the book and slid it into the saddlebag.

Cole kept the palomino at a steady trot until he stopped atop a rise that held a better view of what was ahead. From the top of the hill, numerous others yet to pass were all he could see. The afternoon light became consumed by the dark clouds building in the north. Occasional drops pelted his face, blown by the fury of the coming storm. He dipped his head so the hat shielded his face, then nudged his horse down the slope.

More dirt than grass brought Cole out of the saddle. He crouched, taking slow steps and scanning the ground for tracks. Some signs of heavy animals appeared, maybe elk or deer passing as they grazed. He wasn't looking for cloven hooves. More steps only produced impatience. The wind snapped in his face. A peek at the clouds signaled the threat of a storm. If there were tracks to find, rain would soon wash them away. He took a long breath and huffed it out. A better reason to stop riding may be over the next rise. He stepped into the stirrup.

Raindrops pelted his face like stones. He reined in the palomino and untied his bedroll to unfurl the canvas slicker. Once on the horse, he tucked the hat down firmly on his brow. The wind-driven rain brought to mind one of his ma's most trusted pieces of advice: Big drops don't last long.

However, the rain fell with enough fury to change the dirt into mud. He continued on the same line in hopes of sighting anything out of the ordinary despite the continual drips falling from the hat brim.

More than a mile later, the rain let up as his ma's wisdom predicted. As the storm passed, it took some of his spirit along. The sky still was covered with puffy gray clouds. The wind still howled as if blown by the devil himself. Gusts frequently interrupted the palomino's step. It whistled through the bluffs and buttes that obscured his view. If he was to find the trail, he'd have to cover every inch for signs, even if it meant retracing the same ground and spending hours or days.

He stopped the horse, placed one hand over the other on the horn, and pondered what course to take next. A glance above told him he had three or four hours of daylight at best. How he spent that time was the dilemma before him. Indecision nailed him in place for several minutes, fueling the frustration burning at his gut. A single raindrop struck his cheek.

Another peek above and a scan of the sky proved it was just a lonesome stray. However, as he searched for the cloud that dropped it, he glimpsed a tall rocky butte. A quick comparison with the others showed it to be the highest point. No more than two miles ahead, it would give him the best line of sight.

Once off the palomino, he bent at the waist for balance and took slow steps up the rain-slick rock, careful of each place he put his boot. The wind, although mild on the ground, now felt like a giant with a grip of his shoulders, ready to hurl him to the ground. He gauged the distance to the ground below at better than five hundred feet and maybe as much as a thousand — he couldn't focus on the smaller rocks at the bottom. He closed his eyes for a moment to calm his nerves — he knew he wouldn't survive a fall from either height.

The higher he went, the more rolling hills he'd already passed came into view and the narrower the place to make his next step. He eased down to sit on the massive boulder and scooted his backside inch by inch until he was within a foot of the edge.

Secure with his balance, he peered into the distance in all directions. Most of what he saw, he'd already seen. More grass with a spattering of trees filled the scene from both the south and east. A cautious glance behind him to the north showed more escarpments like the one he was on, and even farther away in the hazy horizon he could make out snowcapped mountains. It was the same range extending all the way south to Colorado. After a moment's reflection, he came to the realization that the place he was in today would be covered in snow in a month's time.

He spun around almost full circle to view the west. The plain rose and fell as far as he could see. Trees stood bunched in a grove maybe as far as a mile or two. Their presence was a sign of some water flow, whether atop the ground or below it. It was a good sign to follow, since no signs of riders were evident. As careful as he began, he scooted his rear inch by inch backward down the slope until he reached the bottom. Mounting his horse, he took off.

He kept the palomino at a lope. Soon, the trees appeared to be a mesh of oak, fir, and tall pines. The line extended beyond the crest of the far hill. As he came near, he placed his right palm on the Colt. While watching for any movement, he slowed the horse and drew the pistol. He glanced down and saw some tracks, but none appeared to be made from riders. Uncomfortable with so many tree trunks a shooter could hide behind, he stayed in the saddle until he had a reason to dismount.

Slowly, he steered the horse into the woods, dodging low limbs while scanning left and right. Weaving a path between the trees, he found nothing. Once out of the trees and sure he'd left nothing behind to spot or shoot at, he rode parallel to the stretch of trees up to the crest of the hill, routinely casting a wary eye into the woods.

Once he was atop the hill, Cole slowed the palomino long enough to scan the new ground. The wavy terrain sloped to the left. As he looked in that direction, a ridgeline of exposed rock jutted out of the hill. He nudged the horse and followed the grade. The farther he went, the taller the ridge extended above the ground until he came level about fifty feet below the top of the rocks. Now thin clouds presented a haze over the western sun, easing its effect on his eyes. However, a light glare prevented him from focusing on a dark structure silhouetted in the distance. He put his hand on the butt of the Colt and rode toward the object.

As he neared, the shape appeared more like a tree. His heart sank a little when he dismounted to concentrate on the figure. He took the spyglass from the saddlebag. With a firm stance, he squinted into the eyehole and focused. The shape took form. A long, dangling figure. A dark figure. A man's body. Choate.

He dropped the spyglass and fell to his knees as if a gut punch had sucked out his very soul. Shoulders drooped, not taking his eyes off the sight, he couldn't breathe. It couldn't be. Not after all this.

First in small gulps, then quick pants, he sucked wind back into his lungs. Rage filled him. He rose from his knees, seized the horn, and flung his leg over the saddle. With a full kick, he sent the palomino into a gallop at the tree.

The cool air whipped across his face with the speed, watering his eyes, blurring his vision. A depression in the land would have sent him flying off the saddle if not for the furious grasp of the reins and horn. As hooves flew across the small plain, the couldn't take his eyes off the figure of his friend. As the land rose to the top of the crest, the tree came into clear focus.

He reined in hard, to the complaining whinnies of the palomino. He slid off the saddle. There, beneath the body of the half-breed, Cole stood stiff, almost in a trance at the sight before him that he had never truly prepared himself to see.

His blood rushing through his veins, he drew the Bowie knife and went to where the rope was tied to a lower branch. He hugged the legs to break the fall and sliced through the rope. The weight fell upon his shoulder. He caught his balance and did his best to ease himself to a knee and put the body to a gentle rest.

He cut away the noose from the neck. The motion brought movement from his friend.

"Choate? Choate!" His cries appeared to bring life back into the body. He screamed louder. "Choate!"

Gurgling erupted from the man's throat. Cole looked for a wound. Only a dark bruise around the neck could be seen. He cupped the head in his left hand. There was no loose movement. The neck wasn't broken. His friend had been strangled by the knots.

Panicking over what to do next, he went to the saddle and ripped the canteen from the gear, then raced back to kneel beside the body. He poured water into the mouth, dousing the lips in his haste.

"Choate. Can you hear me?" Cole looked into nearly closed eyes. His blood boiling, he shook the shoulders, instantly realizing he may be causing more harm. "Choate, talk to me. Talk to me, you black half-breed bastard son of a bitch." As he screamed, he saw the flutter of the eyelids. "That's it. Just breathe a little. You're going to be all right."

The eyelids opened halfway, but no life appeared behind them. Again, he poured water into the lips, gently this time, trying to spark a reaction. There was none.

"You just rest. I'm going to get you home. We'll wait a spell. Until you think you can stand to be in a saddle for a time."

Despite his urgings, there was no response. No twitch. No sound. Cole put his head to Choate's chest. He squeezed his eyes shut, concentrating to hear the most faint of beats. There was nothing coming from inside. He flung his hat to the side and pressed his hands hard against the breast. As he'd done with folks who sucked in water, he pushed against the ribs to try to force in breath.

"Come on, Choate. I know you're in there. Breathe, you half-breed devil." He pushed hard, jolting the body back and forth. "You're too damn tough to die. Not like this. You didn't die on that reservation. You didn't die on that mountain in Idaho." The more he tried, the less desire his own muscles could push. There was no life left in his friend.

Exhausted more from the disappointment than the effort, he laid his brow against the chest. After a few moments, he lifted his head to stare into the lifeless, half-open eyelids.

"I'm sorry, old friend," he whispered. "I'm sorry I didn't come faster." He collapsed to sit on his left hip. Arms drooped by his side, he stared at the body while the wind howled in his ears.

It was the wind whipping in his face that brought him from the trance and turned him toward the north. The clouds were still thick. Daylight wouldn't be long in lasting. The nag of necessity finally brought him to his feet. There was a burying that needed to be done.

He went to his horse. He had no tool to dig a grave. The spade used to dig fire pits had been lost with the bay. Not knowing the distance to the next town, he pondered

whether to bring the body with him or
continue his search. While he considered
the effort needed, his attention wandered to
the ground. A mark in the dirt caught his
eye. He knelt next to it. Brushing the grass
from his view, there he saw a horseshoe
print, a flawed spur at the top. A few feet
away lay another.

CHAPTER NINETEEN

Cold surrounded Richard. The chill shook his shoulders and the reflex opened his eyes. The dank interior of a shanty slowly came into focus. Single planks stood on end acted as walls. The gaps between the boards were at least big enough to poke a finger through, and some the whole hand. The roof wasn't any better. A small pit dug out in the center of the dirt floor acted as a hearth. The cold ashes lay beneath a wide-mouthed tin pipe functioning as a chimney.

He rose to sit up, but the pounding pain at the back of his head reminded him of his last conscious thoughts of their approach to this place atop a grassy hillside. His hands were bound in front with coarse twine, as were his legs. The air was heavy and moist. He peeked between the planks. The grass outside was green, long, and leafy. However, thick gray clouds hung low. It seemed winter wouldn't be long in making its arrival. A lone leafless tree stood at the edge of the sloping horizon. Richard's heart pounded as he observed a rope slung over a high limb. At the end was a noose.

He strained against the bounds while seeing Coy Dallas for the first time returning to the shanty. The knots held stiff. His tired muscles couldn't produce any slack. If he could get to his feet, maybe he could run, or hop, anything to escape. However, within seconds, the outlaw leader entered through the front where there was no door.

"You're awake," Dallas greeted with some surprise and sly glee. "Good. That will make it better."

"Make what better? What do you plan to do?"

Dallas paused and in a casual manner glanced outside at the tree. "I'm planning on leaving. Alone."

Richard's chest squeezed out all breath. He panted as his eyes dared glance at the tree once more. Thoughts of struggling against the binding sank away when fear seized his body. The sound of scraping turned his attention back to Dallas.

Bent over the fire pit, the outlaw leader shoved away the ashes with constant strokes. After most of the debris was gone, he rapped his knuckles against a hollow metal plate. With both arms outreached, he gripped the plate's ends and lifted. He tossed the plate aside and drew out canvas bags in each hand, all the while hooting a satisfied laugh.

At first confused, Richard watched as the answers to questions became apparent. "That's why you're here."

Dallas glanced briefly at him but didn't stop hauling more bags of loot from the hole. "What's that you're saying?"

"The reason you've come this far," Richard barked. "To recover what you've robbed. That's been the reason all along. That's the reason the Pinkertons were so anxious to find you. To get back the money that you stole."

Dallas wasn't alarmed by the accusation. Instead, he continued pulling the last three bags out and then nodded. "Yep."

"This trail of murder — it's all been for the money?"

Dallas turned about and slid two of the canvas bags into a saddlebag. "Seeing how it don't make much difference what I tell you, I will say that what I did to those people was only what they wanted done to me." The confession seemed sincere.

"Revenge," Richard muttered. "You killed those jury members and the judge to gain it before you came for your money."

Dallas's mood instantly brightened. "I haven't killed them all. Not yet." He went about stowing two more bags.

"So those still left on the jury — they'll live in fear of you."

Busy with his work, Dallas talked as he packed. "Well, we just might let them live in that fear a little longer."

"Why?" Suddenly, the answer to his own hasty question came. "So you can escape." Dallas's sly smile confirmed the truth. "That's how you've planned it. All this time."

"You see," said the bandit leader, "it don't make too much sense to kill all of them."

Richard shrank at the suggestion, but he couldn't be so relieved as to not look outside at the tree. "And so you will let me live, too." The suggestion was met by a smile, then gradually a shake of the head. "But why? I am a writer. I can make you famous."

Dallas approached him. "Already got too many folks knowing about me as it is." He stepped clumsily on the knobbed dirt. Richard cowered from his grasp, but the planked wall wouldn't allow further retreat.

"Wait," he said, attempting to bargain, yet with nothing of value to sell. "You don't have to kill me." He hoped the plea would be enough to slow the man's tug. Dallas kept about his plan, grabbing Richard's shoulders. With bound hands, there was nothing he could do but twist to free himself, if only for a moment — further angering Dallas.

"Keep still. Just relax and this won't hurt a bit."

"I'll pay you," Richard offered. "I have money. My wife's family has wealth. I'll pay anything you want. A thousand dollars? Two? Ten? If you'll allow me to live, you can make good your escape." Dallas dragged him across the dirt back first. Richard peeked through the boards at the lonesome tree with the noose dangling in wait. "Please don't do this. You don't have to kill me. I'll not tell a soul where you went." The certainty of his encroaching death dug through his spirit. He sobbed like a child but felt no shame. "Why do you have to hang me? I've done nothing to harm you."

"Well," Dallas replied in an almost giddy manner, "there's just something about seeing people swinging from a limb that gets a man's pride swelling." He grunted as he yanked Richard's weight. "Kind of a sign that a man ain't to be trifled with. Sends a pert clear message. And while they're looking for me, I'll be long gone. Maybe settling in the East. Could be where you lived."

Richard choked through his tears, swallowing saliva just to talk, constantly casting an eye between the boards. "I beg you. Please, if you are to kill me, please, not like this. Not in this way."

The request was met with laughter. "What's the matter? Too good to swing?"

Dallas heaved backward once more, bringing both of them in line with the doorway. Richard couldn't bring himself to peer at his destiny, but the abrupt release of Dallas's hands drew his attention to the outside.

Clay Cole sat astride his mount between the tree and the shanty.

Richard exhaled in jubilant shock.

For more than a moment, Cole stared at both of them. He didn't appear angry or relieved, only steadfast in his steady glare. Dallas stood above Richard as if he was stunned, frozen stiff by the surprise, his pistol in the loose holster left by the doorway.

Cole pulled back his coat in a slow, deliberate motion.

Dallas raised his arms. "That badge is no good here."

With the same motion, Cole drew the Colt.

"I ain't armed," Dallas yelled.

Cole cocked the hammer, aiming the pistol with his outstretched right arm.

Dallas screamed louder. "Ain't you listening?"

The blast rang out. Richard cringed, seeing the puff of smoke from the Colt, hearing Dallas stumble backward over the saddlebags filled with money to collapse against the back wall planks. The bullet hole bled in the center of Dallas's chest. As his features were sapped of life, a word leaked through his lips:

"Rainmaker."

CHAPTER TWENTY

The day's labor stood complete. The thick limbs, shaved of branches, were firm and erect as support posts. Rope bound them to the resting bed in place as a platform. It was a structure sure to withstand the harsh winds from the north. Cole gazed upon his work but took no pride in having built it.

Silent Owl stood stoic despite wiping a stray tear trailing down her cheek. She stared at the resting place of her man. Cole didn't feel welcome to stand near. It was his presence in her world that had brought this. He stepped back, hat from his head, and looked upon his friend against the cold gray clouds.

Words never came easy to him. For the first time that he could remember, he took comfort in not knowing what to say. He wasn't sure she would know what he meant even if he were to attempt to do so. Sermons for the dead were not his business.

In a muted tone, she mouthed what ceremony her tribe had taught her. Respect made him stand firm. Whatever message she was sending above was better than he could muster. As she chanted, he thought not about the marker staked in the ground but the one carved into his soul.

A long time past, he was just a young trooper anxious to make his mark in or maybe against the world. Alone, with parents gone to the great beyond, he thought it his right to strike at all that gave him such reason to grieve. The Army put his hatred to use clearing out Indians from desired land. It was after his stretch was up that his life changed, and he didn't even see it coming. A colored man with spotty whiskers gave him an invite to join him on the open range. Without further prospects, he took up the offer and rode with a sage old man named Jenks.

During the near five-year ride, he soaked up some of the knowledge not just of why the wind blows the way it does, but why some people do also. Without kin of his own, he took to those he met on the endless trail from town to town.

Following the black man caused him to meet up with the likes of Hickok, a better pistol shot dead drunk than most men were stone sober. He didn't think much of the gunman at first, but since the legend's death he had understood why the man seemed to walk in silent pain. It was the same loneliness for the past he himself carried now.

Not long after parting from the same path, he found he could make money guiding troopers into the West. Prospects were low and the money was government backed. One of those was Custer. Never much caring for the swagger of the man, he found himself at odds more than once with the boy general. However, they bore an alliance, even if it was uneasy. It was that split in allegiance to commanders that put him on the wrong side of the Little Bighorn River and sent him on this course to free himself from that shroud.

He inhaled the chilly wind.

Jenks had passed on nearly three years ago. Before him now was his mentor's only son. Even though a half-breed, the body still bore the dark skin of his father. Even if it spited him, Choate knew he was from a line of colored men that lived as the whites. He never took to it, even if he made his living from hunting down wanted men for the white man's money. Never did he make the bones of his pa part of his own.

A satisfied grin creased his face as he

looked to the grieving Silent Owl.

As he concentrated on her swollen belly pushing against the skins of her tribal dress, he felt kinship with this cut-apart family. Having known the past of this line, he saw the future and had done what he could to see that it continued.

A glance to the west prodded him to leave Silent Owl alone with her ancestors to plead acceptance for the one she loved. He put on his hat and went to the palomino. He didn't want to disturb her native prayers, but when he checked the cinch on the saddle, he couldn't help a last glance. She had turned her attention to him. Her face never changed. Not a hint of a smile. It wasn't a time to be waving farewells, but he took solace in her silent sign of his passing. That, indeed, he was a part not only of the family of her man, but also of her unborn child.

With a step into the stirrup, he swung his leg over the horse and settled into the saddle. Before any second thoughts entered his head to slow him, he turned the palomino west, mustering all the will possible not to glance to the side as he passed, or behind from where he left, but ahead, where he was yet to go.

Richard crossed the main street of Copper

Springs and stepped on the boardwalk. After two weeks of lying on his back in bed, the sunshine warming his face on the chilly day felt good. He took a few steps before he saw the barred windows. He stopped at the door to take a deep breath and let it out before turning the knob.

"Well," greeted Sheriff Stillman with a wide smile, "I see you got some good vittles in you. You look like a new man since the last I saw you. How you feeling?"

Richard returned the smile and nodded. "Much better, thank you."

"You look it. Maybe more than a mite thinner, but still good just the same. I'm glad for you." Stillman reclined in his chair. The two men looked into each other's eyes for a moment. Richard stood unsure of what polite small talk to say next, but his tongue was stuck with a slim shroud of shame. He didn't care to bring more notice to his ordeal, nor did he care for any sympathy. He was alive. It was all the notoriety he wanted. Finally, he gathered the courage to broach the subject of his visit. "I was told at the hotel that you may have some of my belongings."

Reminded with surprise, Stillman reached for the lower desk drawer. "Yes, sir. You were told right." He removed a large envelope and tossed it on the desktop. "He left these."

"He?"

The two men met eyes and paused. Stillman nodded. "Him."

Richard lifted the flap of the envelope and slid the contents onto the desk. The leather-bound journal spilled onto the wood top followed by the gold-chained pocket watch. He picked it up and opened it. There, as always, was beloved Emily, smiling as she had that day. Richard closed his eyes and inhaled deeply in relief. His world was returning. All his safe and stable surroundings began once again wrapping around his shoulders like a warm blanket. He once thought he'd lost them. His wife's smile brought them back like a magnet.

From the corner of his eye he saw the sheriff smiling from the chair. "When did he leave these?" asked Richard.

The lawman rolled his eyes to the ceiling. "Ah, must be more than a week. Yup, near close to two by now. The same day he brought you to town."

The news was disappointing. "I wanted to thank him personally for saving my life. Did he mention where he might be going?"

"Not for sure," Stillman answered with a shake of his head. "When he left here, he went to take Choate's body back to his place." Both men paused for a moment in remembrance of their friend. "Yeah, I was so sorry to see that half-breed across that saddle." Stillman looked to Richard again. "He said he was taking him to be buried, or whatever them Crow do. Didn't say much when he rode off. Just shook my hand and told me to put in for the reward on Dallas. When it comes in, I'm to give it to the squaw Choate took in. I guess he kept a woman there. I never knew he had one. You know how them injuns are. Don't speak much English, and that they do, ain't about no personal things. I guess it ain't no harm. Not being Christian and all."

Richard breathed a glimmer of relief. He hadn't known the half-breed personally, but he had heard nothing but good mentioned in his memory. The short time they were together didn't provide much to remember. It was pleasing to learn that family, if it could be rightly considered so, would be taken care of as part of his work. A shudder ran through Richard's spine. "You are going to see that she gets the money, aren't you?"

Stillman's jaw dropped, as if he were being accused of a crime. His face lightened, followed by a quick, short chortle. "Choate was my friend. Besides, I don't want the

Rainmaker on my trail if he was to hear about it. No sir. Not after he brought in Coy Dallas with a bullet through the heart. I wouldn't enjoy one nickel's worth of pleasure from it. I plan to do just as I was told."

Richard nodded appreciation at the sheriff's intentions. He noticed the marshal badge alone on the corner of the desk. "Did he say where he might be going after?"

Stillman shook his head. "Ain't no telling. If'n I had to reckon a guess, I'd say he was going west." The shake of the head turned into a nod. "Asked a heap of questions about that red-haired gal out of California. Could be headed to San Francisco. Easy for a man with his reputation to get himself lost in a big city such as that, if you know what I mean."

Richard raised a brow himself. Conversations concerning the Australian singer came to mind. It was a definite possibility. "And you as the law had no qualm with him leaving your custody?"

With palms open, Stillman shook his head again. "I had no papers against him. He was here on Choate's business. With the half-breed dead, I had no charges to keep him here. And it weren't like I was trying to find none, either. As far as I'm concerned, he is a free man."

Richard's heart sank when he peered onto the smudged pages. The words, his words, blurred by the diluted lead smeared by the wet elements. Barely a word was decipherable. A single chuckle bubbled from his mouth. This was the last casualty of his long ordeal.

"So, what you going to do with yourself now?"

Stillman's question was an interesting one. Up until that moment, Richard hadn't considered his prospects. With the discovery of his ruined journal, there was little to pin his hopes on. It would be a long journey east. Emily's smile would be waiting, but only due to his safe return. He imagined her look of horror when he recounted the tale of his near death at the hands of Coy Dallas. There was little doubt she would use the experience to convince him to relent in his ambitions of being a writer and pursue more respectable vocations.

"I'm not sure." Richard peeked at the leather-bound journal. "It would seem that all my work was for nothing."

"Why you say that?"

He slapped the book shut. "My notes are a shambles. I couldn't form them into any shape for a book." The loud tone pierced his own ears, so he paused to calm his nerves and his voice. "It might be for the best. There've already been numerous books written about the famous Wild Bill Hickok. I suppose one more wouldn't gather much interest to sell many copies." He sighed the familiar lament with a slight grin. "No, I am destined to failure. I will return to Chicago and toil in the haberdasheries selling shirts and acting the servant to heal the complaints of the snobbish customer."

The diatribe appeared to confuse Sheriff Hap Stillman. "If that sounds like you're giving up, seems a shame. I see you're a fellow with a lot of want. Just seems you haven't found what to give that folks need." He arched a thumb to the west. "Come to think of it, he thought so, too. He told me to tell you to write your book."

Richard was about to repeat all the reasons that the task was impossible, when his mind seized his tongue. All the story he'd researched was lost, save the one he had lived himself. A grin grew across his face. New York City may have learned all they cared to about Wild Bill Hickok. However, there was another man they knew nothing about.

Richard's eyes followed the lead of the sheriff's thumb, turning his head to the west. He couldn't keep his grin from blossoming into a gleaming smile.

ABOUT THE AUTHOR

Tim McGuire is the author of Western and Thriller fiction. He lives in Grand Prairie, Texas. To learn more about the author, go to his website at www.timmcguire.com.

The employees of Thorndike Press hope you have enjoyed this Large Print book. All our Thorndike and Wheeler Large Print titles are designed for easy reading, and all our books are made to last. Other Thorndike Press Large Print books are available at your library, through selected bookstores, or directly from us.

For information about titles, please call:

(800) 223-1244

or visit our Web site at:

www.gale.com/thorndike
www.gale.com/wheeler

To share your comments, please write:

Publisher
Thorndike Press
295 Kennedy Memorial Drive
Waterville, ME 04901